BRENDA JACKSON

BACHELOR UNBOUND

D0011802

⬡ **HARLEQUIN**® KIMANI™ ROMANCE

Recycling programs for this product may not exist in your area.

ISBN-13: 978-1-335-21694-6

Bachelor Unbound

Copyright © 2018 by Brenda Streater Jackson

HARLEQUIN®
™ www.Harlequin.com

Printed in U.S.A.

Brenda Jackson is a *New York Times* bestselling author of more than one hundred romance titles. Brenda married her childhood sweetheart, Gerald, and has two sons. She lives in Jacksonville, Florida. She divides her time between family, writing and traveling. Email Brenda at authorbrendajackson@gmail.com or visit her on her website at brendajackson.net.

Books by Brenda Jackson

Harlequin Kimani Romance

Forged of Steele

Hidden Pleasures
Possessed by Passion
A Steele for Christmas
Private Arrangements

* * *

Bachelors in Demand

Bachelor Untamed
Bachelor Unleashed
Bachelor Undone
Bachelor Unclaimed
Bachelor Unforgiving
Bachelor Unbound

Visit the Author Profile page
at Harlequin.com for more titles.

Let us not love with words or speech
but with actions and in truth.
—*1 John* 3:18

To the man who will forever be the love of my life
and the wind beneath my wings, Gerald Jackson, Sr.

To all my readers who have waited patiently
for Zion's story, this book is for you.

To my sons, Gerald Jr. and Brandon. Please continue
to make me and your dad proud. I love you guys.

To my family and friends
who continue to support me in all that I do.

Chapter 1

"Where the hell are you, Z?"

Zion Blackstone waited in Baggage Claim for his luggage to appear on the conveyor belt. Once his flight from Rome had landed, getting through Customs had been a monumental nightmare. "I'm in the States."

"I know that. But where?" York Ellis asked in a tone that suggested he had every right to know Zion's whereabouts.

"Just landed in LA and I'm still at the airport," Zion said, glancing around at all the travelers hurrying to and fro.

"What are you doing in Los Angeles?"

Zion could easily tell York that he'd gotten one question answered and not to try his luck for two, but figured it wouldn't do any good. He had five godbrothers, and Zion was used to them trying to keep up with him. That was the price you paid when you were the youngest in the group.

Most of his friends knew the story of how over forty years ago, while attending college at Morehouse in Atlanta, six guys had become best friends. On graduation day they had made a pact to stay in touch by becoming godfathers to each other's children, and that the firstborn sons' names would start with the letters *U* through *Z*. And that was how Uriel Lassiter, Virgil Bougard, Winston Coltrane, Xavier Kane, York Ellis and Zion Blackstone had come to have their names and their connections. From the time they were babies it had been drilled into them that as godbrothers they were to have each other's backs.

York was an ex-cop turned high-tech security expert and was programmed to ask a lot of questions. And unfortunately for Zion, York was the most overly protective of the godbrothers. Zion recalled that when he'd made the decision to travel abroad for a year, it had been York who'd taken it upon himself to join him. At the time both Zion and York had demons to fight, and instead of staying put and dealing with them, they'd hauled ass. After that year York had returned to the States ready to get his shit together and conquer his demons, but Zion wasn't ready. Now, eight years later, he still wasn't ready.

"Z?"

Zion figured if he didn't answer York, he would eventually get calls from U, V, W and X, namely Uriel, Virgil, Winston and Xavier. Over the years, he and his godbrothers had shortened their names for each other to just the first letter. Whenever they used the full first name it was a strong indication they were getting annoyed or already there.

"The reason I'm in LA, *York*, is because I'm on my way to the home of Levy Michaels."

"Levy Michaels, the actor?"

"Yes." And because he knew what York's next question would be, he said, "He's commissioned me to design a unique set of jewelry for his daughter's twenty-fifth birthday."

"Celine Michaels?"

"Yes."

Zion wasn't surprised York knew the name of Levy's daughter when her face was so often plastered across magazines and tabloids. Some referred to her as the "jet-setting queen."

Whenever Zion was commissioned to make personal jewelry pieces, he liked getting to know the individual and determining his or her personality, in order to make that piece of jewelry unique. It was his way of offering his clients the opportunity to provide input on the style or stone they preferred, and any specific elements they wanted included in the design. In the end, what they got was a Zion original, a distinctively created piece of jewelry representing his finest custom work.

"Do you plan to return to the States next month and stay through the holidays?" York asked.

In the past, during the holidays he would return to the States from Rome so the six of them could get together at a designated location. Uriel, Virgil and Xavier lived in Charlotte, North Carolina. Winston was presently living in Australia, and York made his home in New York. A lot had changed over the past few years. His godbrothers were no longer happy-go-lucky, never-intending-to-marry bachelors. U, V, W, X and Y were now all married men.

Zion was the lone bachelor left of the Bachelors in Demand Guarded Hearts Club, a club they'd founded a few years ago. At the time all six godbrothers had been going through their own personal hell with women and had made a pledge to remain single forever, referring to themselves as bachelors in demand. They were in demand of their futures without a permanent woman in it. Definitely never a wife. Now five had defected and Zion was determined to keep the club going, no matter what. He'd met a few single men who expressed interest, but as of yet, no one had submitted membership applications.

"Z? You still there?"

York's question grabbed Zion's attention again. "Yes, I'm still here, and no, I won't be joining you guys for the holidays this year. I'll be busy working on the Michaels jewelry."

"When is his daughter's birthday?"

"April."

"This is October. You have plenty of time."

"What I'll be designing is jewelry made of a very unique gemstone just for her. Although I'm skipping the holidays this year, I plan to return for W's homecoming party in February." Winston, a marine biologist, and his wife, Ainsley, had been living in Australia for the past three years while Winston worked on some special project dealing with sea turtles.

"You'd better be there. It's time you stopped acting like a recluse."

Zion didn't mind acting like a recluse. In fact, he rather enjoyed it and preferred living a quiet life and not being in the limelight. He'd become an overnight sensation after being selected as the former First Lady's personal jeweler. The next thing he knew, his face was appearing on the covers of notable magazines and his privacy was invaded in a way that was unacceptable to him. He figured others might like getting such publicity, but not him. He liked his privacy and had no problem being referred to as a loner or, like Y had said, even a recluse.

When Zion saw his luggage, he said, "Okay, Y, I see

my bags. I'm sure I'll be talking to you again before I return to Rome."

"You can't run forever, Z."

Zion drew in a deep breath. Leave it to York to come out and say what the others were thinking. But then, Uriel had expressed that same sentiment a few years ago. Zion had denied it then and he would deny it now. "I'm no longer running, York. I just prefer simplicity to chaos. Truth to lies. Honesty to deception."

"Then maybe it's time for you to find out what's the truth and what's a lie."

More than once he'd told himself it was time. Then he would quickly decide to just leave well enough alone. "I got to go, York."

"I'll let the others know I talked to you so they won't call and pester you," York said.

"Like you're doing?"

"Hey, I don't pester," his godbrother exclaimed.

"Whatever. How's Darcy?" York had called everyone a couple of months ago to announce that he and Darcy were expecting. Xavier and his wife, Farrah, had had their second child earlier that year. Marriage and then babies, Zion thought. What a vicious cycle.

"Darcy is doing fine now that morning sickness has passed. We're counting the days until the baby gets here."

Zion shook his head. It was hard to believe that five of what used to be die-hard bachelors had fallen in love and fallen hard. That was the bad thing. The good thing was that Zion thought the women they'd fallen in love with were ultra-special. He couldn't help but love them for making his godbrothers happy. "Give her my love. Now let me go grab my bags. I'll talk to you later."

He clicked off the phone and headed toward the conveyor belt.

* * *

"You can be a little more appreciative, you know."

Celine Michaels glanced up from her breakfast plate and met her father's gaze. He was annoyed with her. What else was new? They rarely saw eye to eye on anything. He didn't understand her, and quite frankly, most of the time she didn't understand him. "I *am* appreciative, Dad, but…"

"But what?"

She would try to explain, although she knew it really was no use. They'd had this conversation, or ones pretty similar, plenty of times. "With the money you're spending on jewelry for my birthday, just think of all the homeless people that could be clothed, fed and housed."

She watched him roll his eyes. "Not my problem and neither is it yours. If they're out there on the streets that means they want to be out there."

"That's not true," she said, placing her fork down. She always got annoyed with his I-don't-give-a-damn attitude. "Anyone can fall on hard times."

"True, and anyone can pull themselves up by the bootstraps, too. I wasn't born rich, you know, but I worked my tail off to get what I have, what I can give to you, my only child. My concern is not about the person out there looking for a handout."

He might not be concerned, but she was. That was one of the reasons, while still in college, she'd founded Second Chances, without his knowledge. He would flip if he knew she was CEO of one of the most notable charities in the city, and that she had used a lot of *his* money to do it. It was money he thought he was giving her to jet all over the world or do something equally as frivolous, like spend a day shopping on Rodeo Drive. Even though she was nearing twenty-five, he still gave her a generous monthly allowance. Then there was the trust fund from her maternal grandparents that she'd received at age twenty-two. Those monies, along with the funds her father had frequently sent her while she attended college, had fed and bedded a lot of homeless people.

"Forget I suggested it," she said, picking up her fork again.

"I will. In fact, I've forgotten already."

Celine narrowed her eyes at her father, glad most people would tell her that she'd gotten her ways from her mother and not him. She would admit he looked good for his age. He was almost sixty and could pass for a man ten years younger. He carried his age well, and on top of that, he was physically fit. No reason he shouldn't be, when he had a private gym in their home and a personal trainer who came practically every day.

She knew his story, since she'd heard it a number of times. He had arrived in Hollywood over thirty years ago, right out of college. While working at a men's clothing store he'd been discovered by some director looking for a handsome face to be an extra in a movie, and thought he fit the bill. Now, over twenty movies later, her dad was trying his hand at producing.

"Now that we have that cleared up, let's get back to your birthday gift. He will be arriving today and staying with us for the weekend."

She lifted a brow. "Who?" She hoped not Nikon Anastas, Hollywood's latest heartthrob. For months he'd been connecting his name with hers for a publicity stunt, with her father's blessing. She'd gone along with it just to get her dad off her back.

"Zion Blackstone, the jewelry designer," he said, before taking a sip of his coffee.

Celine didn't say anything for a minute. No matter how many times she'd told her father not to waste his money on her, he refused to listen. "Why is he coming here?" she asked. From what she'd heard, the man was practically a recluse, preferring to stay out of the limelight to design all that jewelry that had made him rich and famous.

"He wants to get to know you."

She lifted a brow again. "Why?"

Her father served himself another helping of the delicious meal their cook had prepared. "He needs to know your taste, to make sure he designs the jewelry pieces right."

"Is all this necessary?"

"For the amount of money I'm paying him, it is. I want to make sure it's something you like."

And something flashy that could be seen. There was no doubt in her mind that her father had things all planned. Certain members of the media would be invited to her party to make sure they captured the moment she opened her gift from him. Jewelry by Zion was all the rave, and for publicity, Levy Michaels would do just about anything. Her father loved being in the limelight. Always had, and she figured he always would.

"I won't be here. I'm spending the weekend with Desha," she said. She and Desha had been best friends since junior high school. Desha had gotten a finance degree and was CEO of her own investment firm. Thanks to Desha, Celine's money had grown more than she could have hoped.

Levy frowned. "You need to change those plans. Blackstone will only be here for this weekend."

She started to say that Zion Blackstone could design the jewelry without her input, but she'd decided long ago to pick her battles when it came to her father. "Fine. I will be here," she finally said, rising to her feet. "Now if you will excuse me, I need to call Desha, to let her know of the change in our plans."

Celine walked out the room, thinking that one of these days her father would push her a little too far and she would push back more than she'd ever done. And as for Mr. Zion Blackstone, she wasn't looking forward to spending time with a man who was probably utterly boring. Thanks to him her weekend would be ruined.

Chapter 2

Celine returned home at six o'clock, knowing dinner would be served promptly at seven. She had just enough time to shower and change. If her father had hoped she would hang around to greet Zion Blackstone when he arrived from the airport, he'd been disappointed.

"You're almost late, Miss C."

Celine couldn't help but grin at the older woman who'd greeted her at the door. Aggie had worked in the Michaels household since Celine's parents had married, and before that in her maternal grandparents' employ. She had been her mother's nanny and had followed her when she'd gotten married. Aggie was one of two in the household who knew Celine's secrets. The other was James, the limo driver.

"You have my bathwater ready upstairs, right?"

The older woman returned her grin. "You know I do. I think your father intended for you to return early to help entertain Mr. Blackstone."

Celine rolled her eyes. "I had things to do regarding Second Chances. Where is our houseguest?"

"In the study with your father. Poor fellow. I'm sure he's bored stiff with your father talking about himself."

Celine wanted to throw her head back and laugh but controlled herself. The last thing she wanted was for her father to hear her and know she was back. "You're probably right. What sort of man is Mr. Blackstone?" she asked, heading for the spiral staircase.

Aggie fanned herself. "Wow, missy, he's a hot one for sure. But I'll let you be the judge."

Celine lifted a brow. She'd never known Aggie to refer to any guy as "hot" before. That included Nikon, who wasn't bad looking. "Now you have me curious. I'll be back down soon," she said, rushing up the stairs.

"Make sure you look good. It just might be your lucky night."

Her lucky night for what? Surely Aggie didn't think she would be taken in by a nice-looking face. Just like Aggie knew her secrets, the older woman also knew her past pain. The one Jerome Astor had inflicted. Had it been three years ago? Heading into the fourth? She pushed the memories of her mistake with Jerome out of her mind.

Less than an hour later Celine had showered, dressed and was headed back down the stairs. In good time, she thought, when the study door opened and her father walked out. He was tall, but the man who followed him was even taller. They must have sensed her presence, for they both glanced her way.

She went still when her gaze locked on the stranger she knew to be Zion Blackstone. Aggie hadn't exaggerated one iota. The man was definitely hot. Eye candy so sugary she could develop a sweet tooth just looking at him.

Her heart was pounding hard against her rib cage as

her gaze traveled the full length of him. He had a coppery-brown complexion, eyes resembling chocolate chips and lips so striking she couldn't help but stare at them longer than she should. They were lips any woman would want to run her tongue over in a very indulging lick.

She drew in a sharp breath, not believing that she, of all people, would think something so bold. Reining back her thoughts, which had temporarily gone haywire, she continued her in-depth perusal of Zion Blackstone. Usually she preferred clean-shaven men, but there was something about his neatly trimmed beard covering a square jaw that made him look scrumptious. Then there was the way the dreadlocks flowed past his shoulders, giving him testosterone-driven appeal.

Drop-dead gorgeous seemed too inadequate to describe the man, who was dressed in dark slacks and a tweed jacket that covered broad shoulders and a solid chest. *Breath-hitching hot* was more like it. She actually felt intoxicating sensations rush through her body when she sensed he was undressing her with his eyes.

But then, he could probably make the same claim about her. Like most females, she appreciated a man with good looks and a fantastic body; however, she refused to let one go to her head.

There was a self-assurance about him; he was obviously a man comfortable in any environment. There was no doubt in her mind that whatever room he entered, Zion Blackstone would be front and center. Whether he wanted to or not, he would always stand out.

"Celine. I'm glad you could join us," her father said.

Like I had any other choice. She switched her gaze from Zion Blackstone to her father and lifted a brow. "Of course I was going to join you and Mr. Blackstone, Dad," she said, as she continued walking down the stairs.

After reaching the bottom, she crossed the floor to give Zion her hand, not missing how his concentrated gaze was fixed on every step she took. "Mr. Blackstone. It's nice meeting you," she said, forcing her voice to remain steady.

"Zion, please. It's nice meeting you, as well, and I hope I can call you Celine."

OMG. Why did he also have such a sexy-sounding voice? Deep and husky, with a sensuous bit of throatiness thrown in for good measure. The kind of voice that could croon a woman to sleep. Except the way he was staring down at her with those eyes sent a jolt of sexual awareness straight through to her bones. "Please do," she said, extracting her hand from his.

The brief skin-to-skin encounter had sent even more undefinable sensations rippling through her. She couldn't help wondering if he had felt it the exact moment their hands had touched like she had.

"And how was your day of shopping?"

She forced her attention back to her father. "Great as usual." He would never know her day hadn't been spent on Rodeo Drive like he'd assumed, but instead at a meeting with her executive board at Second Chances, trying to see how they could increase the size of their already-filled-to-capacity facilities.

"My daughter loves spending my money, Zion. And since she's my only child, I love indulging her," Levy Michaels said, smiling proudly. "My motto about money is that you might as well spend it since you can't take any of it with you when you die."

"And he will probably outlive all of us," Celine said, while thinking that although you couldn't take any with you once you were dead, you could certainly share it with the less fortunate while you lived. However, that concept was as nonsensical to her father as the belief of UFOs out in the universe somewhere.

Holding her tongue about that, she turned her attention back to Zion and noticed he was still staring at her with those chocolate eyes. Was he seeing through her facade, or like so many others, did he view her as a spoiled, rich woman whose only goal in life was spending her father's money? A father who happily indulged her to do so. Did it matter what Zion's opinion of her was? She dismissed the sudden thought that it just might if she allowed it. She wouldn't.

"How was your trip, Zion? I understand you came all the way from Rome," she said.

"I did and the flight was interesting. It's not as easy to get through Customs as it used to be, but I managed."

She nodded. Why did he have to smell so good? Whatever cologne he was wearing was definitely his signature scent. A woodsy and masculine aroma. "Have you lived in Rome long?"

"Eight years now."

"Aren't you lucky. I love Rome," she said, walking beside him as they followed her father to the dining room. "It's my favorite place in Italy."

"I believe she fell in love with Rome when I was filming one of my movies there," her father interjected. "It was right after her mother died and she was only twelve. I leased a place there for a year."

"Where in Rome do you live, Zion?" Celine asked. Otherwise her father would start dominating the conversation, and wrestling it from him wouldn't be easy.

"I have a penthouse in the historical center, not far from the Parliament."

She smiled. "I bet I know exactly where you are. You're

in the heart of Rome. Walking distance from Piazza Navona and Via Veneto. The Castel Place."

"That's right," he said, pulling a chair out for her when they reached the dining table. "How did you guess?"

She smiled again. "Because of your notoriety, I figured you would stay someplace with tight security, and that place is known for having one of the tightest. I knew someone, a girlfriend from college, who lived there for a brief time in those same penthouses. They are to die for. How long have you resided there?"

"I've been living in my penthouse for three years now."

She nodded as he took his own seat. "What I enjoy most about the Castel Place are the rooftop terraces."

"I enjoy them, as well."

Zion decided another thing he enjoyed was looking at her. He'd known Celine Michaels was beautiful; he just hadn't known how jaw-dropping gorgeous she was. Whatever jewelry he designed for her would have to complement that beauty in the most exquisite way. It would have to enhance, not distract. His jewelry could never draw attention from the major subject—her. Instead, it would be used to heighten her stunning features.

The gemstones he selected would have to blend in with her skin tone, a perfect shade of russet brown. Then there were her features he intended to capitalize on—almond-shaped eyes the color of pure honey, high cheekbones and a luscious pair of lips. She had such a smooth and graceful neck and he could imagine his necklace adorning it.

She kept her hair in a natural state, with an abundance of curls in a tapered pixie cut. The style embellished her eyes, made them even more noticeable. Even more alluring. No doubt about it, in the looks department Celine Michaels was definitely an attention-getter, and for any man an erection-builder. A high degree of lust would be on any guy's mind when he encountered her.

However, for him there had to be more to a woman than looks and lust. There had to be substance, even with women he didn't intend to keep in his radar for long—which applied to the majority of those he met. Regardless, he couldn't see himself wasting even a second of his time with a woman who lacked substance. A woman who wasn't her own person, who made her way in life depending on others.

Already he was forming an opinion of Celine that wasn't very flattering. What had Levy said about her goal in life? Spending his money. Did she not have any other ambition? Granted, she was wealthy and probably didn't need to work, but what did she do with her time? Was she productive in anything other than shopping and jet-setting around the world to parties? In the study, Levy had actually bragged, as if he was proud Celine had no purpose in life other than spending his money and being under her father's thumb.

From Zion's research he knew she had graduated from Harvard with double master's degrees, in business and psychology. That meant she wasn't an airhead. She had brains. So why wasn't she using them?

His attention was drawn to what she was saying, making another compliment about the place where he lived. In all honesty, what he loved most about the Castel Place was the privacy. What she'd said about the security there was correct. Because of the tight security he didn't have to worry about being hounded by the media or the paparazzi.

He glanced over at Celine and again her beauty stunned him. When he had walked out of the study and turned to see her on the staircase, he'd been captivated by her looks. What had taken him aback even more was his reaction to her. Chemistry, stronger than anything he'd ever felt, had stirred him all the way to his loins. And he was astute enough to know she'd felt it, as well. There was no way she could not have when the chemistry had been so magnetic. The question of the hour was what he intended to do about it. Quickly, he knew the answer: not a damn thing. She wasn't his type and he knew he wouldn't be hers. Besides, he didn't do serious involvements, which was one of his biggest rules. That didn't mean he didn't do involvements, just not the serious type. He had sexual needs like any other man, but knew the women who would and could take care of those needs. The ones who weren't looking for a commitment any more than he was. The ones who knew when he wanted to be left alone.

He would admit there were the fan crazies. Those who figured a night in his bed would get them some trinket or other from Zion. Usually it did. But even with them he was cautious. On his guard against the unexpected. Those with something else up their sleeve—or in most cases, under their dresses—other than a wild night of mind-blowing sex.

Zion made it clear that was all he was into, and any woman who tried to outsmart him with dirty little tricks got tossed out of the hotel room. One from a few months ago quickly came to mind. She had actually tried drugging him after they'd made love. She'd hoped their next round of sex would produce more than off-the-charts orgasms. She had pregnancy in mind and the generous child support payments she figured she would be entitled to as a result of one.

"What made you decide to leave the States to live in Rome?"

He glanced over at Levy. The question had come from him, but out the corner of his eye he could tell Celine was also interested in his response. "A number of reasons," he said, knowing there was no way he would reveal the main one. "I had visited Rome while in college, on one of these exchange trips. I'd stayed there for a semester while learning Italian. I liked the place and the people. When I got the opportunity to live there, I took it."

"But you have family here, right?"

That question had come from Celine, so he switched his gaze to her. His fingers immediately flexed when he suddenly felt the desire to trace one across the smooth skin of her cheeks. He bet it would be soft to the touch. Then there was the urge to push back a wayward curl that had dropped on her forehead. He wished he could ignore the urge to do both, but was finding it difficult.

"Yes, I have family in Atlanta," he finally replied. "My mother died almost nine years ago. It's just me and my dad now."

"So you moved away shortly after your mother passed away?"

Whether she knew it or not, that fact hit a nerve. Somehow, she'd picked up on the timing, which meant she was good when it came to details. Almost too good. "Yes." And that was all he would say about that.

"No other family but your dad?"

He would let her ask all her questions today, because he would ask his tomorrow during his in-depth interview of her as part of the jewelry design process. "I do have a couple of uncles and aunts and several cousins." He paused a minute and added, "I also have five godbrothers, godfathers and godmothers that I'm close to."

"Five? That's a lot of godbrothers."

He chuckled. "Yes, it is. But my father was part of a group of six close friends in college who wanted to stay in touch when they graduated, forty years ago. They figured being godfather to each other's children was a sure-fire way to do it."

"Sounds like fun," Celine said, smiling.

He liked her smile, too damn much. "It's fun whenever the six of us get together. There was a time our godparents dreaded it, though. There was no telling what kind of trouble the six of us would get into."

"Did you get together often while growing up?"

Usually, he didn't talk about his personal life, but for some reason she seemed genuinely interested. "Mostly during the summers and around the holidays. It was on a rotation basis. The goal was to make sure we all got to spend quality time together to build a close relationship with not only each other but our godparents, as well."

She smiled and he thought she had a beautiful pair of lips. "That was a wonderful idea. I bet it worked."

He couldn't help but smile back. "Yes, it did."

Zion was glad when Levy took over the conversation and began asking him about his work, resulting in him switching his focus from Celine to the older man. He was grateful for that. He was determined that when he and Celine got together tomorrow to discuss her preference for jewelry designs, and for him to get a better idea of her personality, he would have more control of himself where she was concerned.

The last thing he intended to happen was for any woman to become more than a passing fancy. Besides, he knew better than to mix business with pleasure. That was another one of his rules.

Chapter 3

"Flowers for you, Miss C," Aggie said, holding the huge vase of roses.

Celine lifted a brow as she came down the stairs, wondering who on earth would be sending her flowers before eight in the morning. When she reached the bottom step she pulled off the card.

Sorry I will miss our date tonight, but I was called away on business. Nikon.

She frowned before glancing back at Aggie. "The flowers are from Nikon. He sent them because he has to cancel our date tonight."

"I didn't know the two of you had a date tonight."

Aggie kept up with her engagements. "Neither did I."

"It was probably an arrangement he and your father made without your input, as usual."

Celine let out a breath of frustration. "I hope you're wrong about that."

"I think you know I'm probably right—otherwise you wouldn't have these flowers. I guess your father forgot to inform you of it."

"He had no right to do that."

Aggie rolled her eyes. "The way I see it, your father will continue to do what he does as long as you don't give him any pushback, Celine. At some point you need to. And while you're at it, you might as well tell him how you're really spending your free time. You're not a child. You'll be twenty-five soon."

Celine bent her head close to Aggie's and said in a low voice, "You know why I handle things the way I do."

"I thought I did, but now I'm not so sure."

"What do you mean by that?" Celine asked, pulling back and glaring at her.

"I'll let you figure it out, but I will say this. You're a lot like your mother, God bless her soul. She was beautiful both inside and out, and she loved people and loved helping them. She had a good heart. She also loved pleasing her parents. In the end, although she did try to stand up to them, she allowed them to control her life by telling her what and who should be a part of it. A part of her future. Now if you will excuse me, I'm going to add more water to this vase of flowers. And Mr. Blackstone is already in the dining room, where you are to join him for breakfast."

Celine's eyes flew up. "He's awake? I'd thought he would sleep late due to jet lag."

"Well, he didn't. In fact, I heard Mr. Blackstone tell your father yesterday that he would be joining you for breakfast. I guess Mr. Michaels conveniently forgot to inform you of that, as well."

"Where is Dad?"

"Out playing golf. He told me before he left that Mr. Blackstone would be your responsibility today."

Celine didn't say anything for a minute and then replied in a low, distraught tone, "I almost lost Dad, Aggie."

"Yes, but the cancer is in remission and has been for almost five years now. You and I both know he's using it to bend you to his will. One day you're going to say it's enough. I hope by then it's not too late and you're not already married off to Nikon Anastas."

Aggie then walked off.

Celine stood there and thought about everything Aggie had said. Although she'd been young and had been sent off to boarding school during the early years of her life, she had known her parents' marriage hadn't been a happy one. She'd overheard conversations between the servants, as well as between her mother and Aggie. She'd discovered years ago that her mother had regretted turning her back on the man she'd truly loved to marry her father, as her parents had ordered her to do.

Her father loved her; Celine was sure of it. But was he intentionally manipulating her love by reminding her how she'd come close to losing him when she'd been in college? Losing one parent was bad enough, but the thought of losing another had freaked her out. However, Aggie was right. Her father couldn't keep trying to control her life.

As far as Nikon was concerned, she honestly wasn't attracted to him. His arrogance was a total turnoff. She merely tolerated him because her father liked the man for some reason, and she'd agreed to be seen with him around town for publicity reasons only. But she was tired of doing even that.

Aggie was right. At some point she needed to have a talk with her father. Knowing she shouldn't keep Zion Blackstone waiting any longer, she headed toward the breakfast room.

* * *

Zion glanced up when he heard footsteps, and saw Celine enter the room. When their gazes connected he noticed a mixture of riotous emotions flicker in her gaze, just for a second. Then they suddenly disappeared and a smile touched her lips. He wondered what that was about.

"Zion, I didn't expect to see you this early," she said, heading for the buffet table where the cooks had set out a variety of breakfast foods. He didn't want to stare, but he couldn't stop gazing at her curvy backside in a pair of jeans, and how her hips swayed with every step she took.

"I'm an early riser, but that doesn't mean you have to be for my benefit. We could have talked over lunch."

She waved off his words as she turned around, and he thought the front looked just as appealing as the back when he took in her beautiful facial features and shapely breasts beneath a yellow blouse. "Meeting with you this morning is fine," she said. "When will you be leaving LA?"

He wondered why she wanted to know. Was his presence putting a dent in her shopping schedule? Her jetting around the globe? "Tomorrow night. I'm booked on a red-eye. After our talk I will sketch a few preliminary designs for you to look at before I leave. Once you select the ones you like, my work here is finished. When I return to Rome the real work begins."

She came to sit across from him at the table and he could inhale her scent. The same one from yesterday that he'd found intoxicating.

"I regret my father had you come all the way from Rome. I'm not hard to please."

"You're not?" he asked, trying to wrap his head around the fact she was saying one thing while he was obviously thinking another.

She glanced over at him, and it was as if she'd suddenly realized her latter statement could easily be taken out of context. She met his gaze and gave him a serious look. "No, I'm not. For me jewelry is a luxury and not a necessity."

Zion continued to hold her gaze while taking a sip of his coffee. He wondered if she knew that when she wore a serious expression it downplayed her dimples but didn't get rid of them altogether. What it produced was a look of irritation that he found so damn arousing he had to shift in his seat to relieve the pressure behind his zipper. "I would hope it's the same with most people," he said.

"Not with my dad. There are certain big-ticket items he sees as a must-have because of the status he's reached in life."

"And you don't?"

"No."

She definitely didn't sound like the picture her father had painted of her yesterday. The girl who loved spending her daddy's money with little to show for it afterward. Maybe the truth of the matter was she had no problem spending her father's money, but only on things she wanted to spend it on.

"So, what do you need to know to design this jewelry of yours?" she asked, interrupting his thoughts.

This jewelry of mine? Zion would overlook her attitude and design the jewelry as he'd been commissioned to do. In the end, whether she appreciated her father's kind gesture or not didn't really concern him. "Do you have any personal tastes?"

She lifted her eyes from her plate, and instinctively, his gaze was drawn to her lips. Beautiful, full lips. It took everything within him not to groan. "Personal tastes?"

Oh, yeah, personal tastes, he thought, wondering what hers were. The intense sexual chemistry that had been between them last night hadn't dimmed any. Why was that realization a hard kick to his testosterone? "Yes, personal tastes…in jewelry. Do you prefer something flashy or something simple?"

"Simple."

He nodded, thinking he would have taken her for a woman who liked flashy. Still, from all accounts she liked being in the spotlight, so during those times she liked being seen, he would make sure any jewelry of his she wore was eye-catching. "You have a very active lifestyle, right?" he asked next.

She took a sip of her coffee. "What does my lifestyle have to do with jewelry?"

He took another sip of his. "A lot, actually. As your designer I want to make sure you fully utilize the jewelry I make for you. Your father has requested a necklace and earrings. I want to make sure the pieces are in keeping with your lifestyle, whether you're out partying, jet-setting around the globe, shopping or whatever else you might do."

She didn't say anything for a minute and then stated, "I'd like them to reflect a simple, laid-back lifestyle. Definitely nothing flashy."

"I find that odd, since you like being in the limelight."

She lifted a brow. "Who doesn't?"

"I don't. I detest it all. Spotlight, limelight, interviews, the paparazzi. I'm a private person and prefer things that way." Not wanting to get off subject, he then asked, "Do you prefer white or yellow gold?"

"Yellow gold."

"Any particular gemstones you prefer?" He found the pensive look that appeared in her eyes rather arousing.

"I know they say diamonds are a girl's best friend, but I love rubies and sapphires."

Zion had been wrong in assuming she was strictly a diamond girl. "Duly noted."

He spent the next half hour asking her additional questions about her tastes and preferences in jewelry. In the end, he believed what she'd said earlier about not being hard to please. He could envision just the style of pieces he wanted to design for her and would make them as unique as she was.

Unique? What exactly he found unique about her, he wasn't sure just yet. Usually when it came to women he grouped them into two types: those who like being pursued and those who preferred doing the pursuing. Problem was, he wasn't sure which group Celine Michaels fell in. Why did he care? There would never be anything developing between them, so it was a moot point. But still, it was hard to look at her and not think of sexual pleasure.

"You didn't write anything down."

He leaned back in his chair. The kitchen staff had come to remove their plates a while ago and had kept their coffee cups filled. "I didn't have to. It's all up here," he said, tapping the side of his head. "Every customer is different and so is their taste. It's my job to design jewelry that's unique to them."

"I can't wait to see what you come up with."

"I think you'll be pleased."

Things suddenly got quiet, but he still noted that intense attraction between them. In a way, he should be flattered that he wasn't losing his touch with women, but he didn't want this one thrown into the mix. His life was already complicated. The last thing he needed was for a woman like her to muddle it even more.

"Do you want to leave here for a while, Zion?"

He wondered what the party girl had in mind. "Leave and go where?"

"A place to have fun and work off nervous energy."

Have fun and work off nervous energy? "And just what do you have in mind, Celine?"

It must have been not only the way he asked the question, but the sound of his voice when he did so, because she shot him a dark look before saying, "Obviously, not what you think."

Zion wondered if he should feel relieved or disappointed. In a way, he felt a little bit of both. "Now you have me curious."

"Curious enough to put yourself in my hands?"

Put himself in her hands. He wondered if she had any idea of the vision those words sent flashing through his head. It was so vivid he had to shift in his chair again.

Too late, she must have figured how that sounded and decided to restate it. "Curious enough to trust me?"

He decided not to tell her that he wasn't capable of trusting any woman. He'd found out the hard way most couldn't be trusted. "Let's just say curious enough to see how we'll have fun and work off nervous energy."

He suddenly saw a glimmer of reluctance in her eyes. But it was too late to back out now because she did have him curious.

"Fine," she said, standing. "Let's meet back here in half an hour."

"Okay," he said, standing as well. "Do I need to dress differently?"

Was he imagining things or was she taking an unnecessary amount of time to run her gaze over his jeans and polo shirt?

She lifted her gaze back to his face. "No, what you're wearing is fine. I'll see you in thirty minutes." And then she quickly walked out of the room.

Chapter 4

"An escape room?" Zion glanced over at Celine when she drove into the parking garage.

She glanced back at him and smiled. "Yes. You ever been to one before?"

He wished she hadn't asked. He recalled a couple of years ago when he and a few of his friends in Rome had gone to one. Being the arrogant male asses they were, with the jacked-up, know-it-all attitudes they had, the eight of them figured they would set a record by escaping from the room with time to spare. Things didn't quite happen that way. Maybe it had been the amount of wine they'd consumed when a couple of the guys had sneaked in several bottles that had basically diluted their brain cells. Whatever the reason, it had them almost beating the walls to get out. The only thing funny about it was when Alessandro hadn't been able to hold his water any longer.

"Yes, I've been to one," he answered, deciding not to provide any details of his one and only time.

"Then you know the rules. There are ten rooms. All locked. The only way to go from room to room is to figure out the clues."

He nodded. "Got it." It would definitely work off nervous energy, although he wasn't sure just how much fun it would be. "Will any others be joining us?" Usually there was a group of people that made up a team.

She glanced over at him as they went inside. "Just me and you. Do you have a problem with it?"

He didn't if she didn't. "No problem."

"Good, because right now we become a team."

They had made it to room ten and now only had to find the last key. He wished he could say getting to this point had been a piece of cake, but that would not be true. As they moved from one room to the next, the clues had gotten more complicated. So far, he'd had the most fun in rooms two and six. Room two had required them to cross a floor that was made of a block of ice, in their bare feet. It had taken him three times before he'd figured the best way to get across was by jumping the distance. However, it had taken him a while to coax Celine to take a leap of faith, literally, and do it that way, as well. Watching her try making the jump made him fully aware of how she looked in her blouse and snug-fitting jeans.

Zion couldn't help but admire how her firm breasts pushed against her top, and the way the denim cupped her backside. He was glad she was too busy concentrating on the jump that she hadn't noticed his arousal. He would be leaving tomorrow and the last thing he wanted was to show any interest in her. The sexual chemistry they were both victims to couldn't be helped as long as they didn't cave in to it and take it further.

He intentionally shifted his concentration to remember

the other rooms they'd been in. In room eight there had been a bunch of numbers on a huge movie screen. They had to come up with five movies that included numbers in the titles, and hope those five were included in the ten chances they got. Luckily for them, *Sixteen Candles*, *Three Men and a Baby*, *Ocean's Eleven*, *Twelve Monkeys* and *Seven* all passed the test. They had the most fun in room five, where they'd had to dance their way out, while making sure their feet touched several hidden marks on the floor.

Now they were in room ten, which held the golden key to getting out. Standing side by side, they faced a huge Scrabble board with the letters *AELBCFIYIE* and the clues "ice," "store," "cat," "fry," "car," "happy," "Friday," "girl," "constellation" and "hand." They had to figure out the phrase in less than fifteen minutes; otherwise, it would go to an even harder phrase.

"We can do this," he said, glancing at Celine and ignoring her doubtful look, the same way he'd been trying to ignore her scent. Whatever perfume she was wearing had her name all over it.

"I don't see any connection with the clues," she said, shaking her head.

"Neither do I," he admitted, standing beside her while studying the board and trying not to let her closeness and scent get to him. "I can see a cat, ice, car and store being connected."

"You can? How?" she asked.

"Because those are the things you can buy at the store."

"What about the word *fry*?" she murmured.

"Well, you can fry a cat."

"What?" She looked at him as if he'd lost his mind.

"Catfish."

"Yes, but you can't fry anything else listed under the clues," she pointed out. "How's our time?"

He checked his watch. "Not good. Less than ten minutes." He watched her move some of the letters around, but nothing made sense.

"And it's not a long phrase, with just ten letters," she said, as she continued to try various groupings.

"No, it's not." He studied the clues again. "I just don't know what connection the others… Friday, girl, hand…"

"Hey, wait a minute. I think we might have something here," she said, excitedly shifting letters again.

He watched her and then checked his watch. They had less than three minutes to go. He glanced over at her and saw the look of excitement on her face. It was crazy, but the quick movement of her hands on the board was a turn-on, because at that moment he could imagine her hands somewhere else.

"There! We got it!"

He blinked, then stared at what she'd come up with: *Bye, Felicia.* He threw his head back and laughed. "Bye, Felicia."

"Yes, the key points that got me thinking were 'ice' for Ice Cube. *Friday* was the movie where the term originated. And the music group Consellation had a song out called 'Felicia' a few years ago."

He nodded. "And 'store' was also a clue, since you go to the store to buy stuff, you usually say 'Bye, Felicia' with a 'hand' motion and Felicia is a 'girl.'"

"Yes. Now hurry! We need to enter it into the computer so the drawer with the golden key will open," she said, quickly moving toward the keyboard.

"We have less than a minute," he said, watching her hands again as they swiftly keyed in the information. The moment she pressed the send key a bugle began playing and balloons began dropping from the ceiling, and then the drawer with the golden key opened for them.

"We did it!" she said, jumping up and down and then

curtsying. He thought the happiness and excitement on her face made her look totally adorable. "We did all ten rooms in less than an hour, Zion!"

She reached out and grabbed him, obviously eager to share the moment. The instant they touched, it seemed something snapped between them. Something neither of them could control. They stood there staring at each other for mere seconds before Zion pulled her into his arms and lowered his mouth to hers.

Celine knew they were swimming in forbidden waters the moment his tongue touched hers, but she was drowning in everything there was about Zion. Things she had tried ignoring and failed miserably. As their tongues tangled, every part of her body seemed to be on some kind of sexual high. Not only was her pulse leaping furiously, but currents that felt like a multitude of itsy-bitsy shock waves began plummeting through her.

There had to be a reason her body was so greedy for Zion's attention. Due to her busy work schedule at Second Chances, she hadn't had much of a social life for a long time. The only person she'd been going out with was Nikon, and he was the last one she wanted to know about her business. He wouldn't hesitate to rush and tell her father everything.

But at this moment, she didn't want to think about Nikon, her father or her charity. She just wanted to concentrate on the mouth that was expertly kissing hers.

There was the way his arms were gripping her. Strong arms. Supportive arms. Masculine arms. And then he shifted his body. Or had she shifted hers? Didn't matter. All that mattered was the way their thighs were touching, denim rubbing against denim, as his jean-clad legs pressed intimately against hers.

There was no telling how long they would have stood

there, locked in each other's arms, devouring each other's mouths, if an announcer hadn't come on the speaker in the room to congratulate them. The sound made Celine jump out of Zion's arms, so fast she almost tripped and fell. He managed to not only keep his balance, but to steady her, as well.

"Careful, Celine."

She swallowed. He was telling her to be careful after he'd nearly gobbled up her mouth. That kiss had bordered on obsession, which made no sense, when they'd met just yesterday. "I'm okay. You can release me now."

"Sure."

But did he have to do it in such a way that suggested he regretted ever having touched her? And then he had the nerve to say, "Sorry about that."

Was he apologizing for the kiss? Why, when it had been something they'd both wanted?

"The announcer said you've won a free visit," he said, cutting into her thoughts.

She looked up at him, feeling annoyed for some reason. Maybe they shouldn't have kissed, but she would not accept his apology for something she'd totally enjoyed. Besides, one kiss didn't hurt anyone. Or did it?

"Are you seeing anyone seriously?" she asked him, suddenly needing to know.

He gave her a look that clearly said it was too late to ask. That made her even more annoyed, and she said, "You initiated the kiss, Zion."

"I never said I didn't. And no, I'm not seriously involved with anyone."

Did that mean he was *casually* involved with someone? Why wouldn't he be? He was a man, wasn't he? And men had a way of stringing a woman along for all the wrong reasons.

"I'm ready to leave now," she stated, trying to keep her anger in check.

"So am I," he said, in a voice that was too cool to suit her.

"Fine." And then she used the golden key to unlock the door.

"Pouting doesn't become you, Celine."

The moment the words left Zion's mouth he regretted saying them. He should have been satisfied with the deafening silence between them, but he wasn't. Nor was he satisfied with how high her chin was lifted in an I'm-really-pissed-off position. And all because of a kiss?

"I am not pouting. I have nothing to pout about."

"Don't you? I apologized for kissing you. What else do you want?"

Luckily, she had come to a traffic light when she jerked her head around to glare at him. "What I don't want is for you to apologize for kissing me."

Zion shook his head. "And just what should I have done?"

"Pretended that you enjoyed it as much as I did."

He looked at her. "I did enjoy it."

"Then why did you apologize?"

The driver behind them honked, letting them know the traffic light had changed. "We need to talk, Celine. Pull into that car wash."

"Why do we need to talk?"

Good question. "It sounds like we're not on the same page about that kiss, that's why."

Instead of pulling into the car wash, she drove a little farther, to an Italian restaurant. She eased into one of the parking spaces and killed the engine. Then she turned to him. "We can talk over lunch. Don't know about you, but after the escape room, I've worked up an appetite."

Not waiting for him to say whether he had worked up

one or not, she got out of the car, and with her curvy ass sashaying all over the place, she entered the restaurant.

Zion followed her while warning bells went off in his head. There was something about Celine Michaels that gave him pause, and he'd be damned, but he just couldn't figure out what it was. All he knew was that if he wasn't careful, she could be his downfall.

He would like to think the only reason they'd kissed was because they'd both been high on adrenaline from trying to beat the clock while figuring out those clues, but he was too smart a man to fall for that excuse. He had kissed her because he had wanted to kiss her, and would even admit that since the first time he'd seen her, studied her mouth, especially those lips, he'd been dying to see how they tasted. Now he knew, and the real thing had been better than the fantasies he'd had in his sleep last night.

Okay, he would admit to those fantasies, no biggie. After all, he was a man and she was a woman. A very attractive woman. He couldn't help it if each time he stared at her lips he could feel blood rushing through him, especially his lower extremities.

A sense of foreboding trickled down his spine. He couldn't help it? The bottom line was that he had no choice but to help it, and to maintain a degree of control, no matter how tempting her mouth was. There was not a woman that Zion Blackstone couldn't resist. Although he'd screwed up at the escape room and let his testosterone overtake his mind, it wouldn't happen again. From here on out, he intended to keep things professional between them.

If that was the case, then the last thing they needed to talk about was a kiss he couldn't seem to forget.

Chapter 5

"I love this place," Celine said, after the waitress had taken their order.

"Evidently."

She lifted her brow at Zion. "And what is that supposed to mean?"

"I can only assume you come here a lot, since you and the owner are on a first-name basis."

Celine took a sip of her water. Zion didn't know that Sergio Moretti was just one of five local restaurant owners who volunteered to give their daily leftovers to homeless people living in Second Chances shelters. "Yes, I do come here a lot."

No need to add that she and Sergio's triplet sons had attended high school together. Not to get sidetracked by the reason he'd wanted to talk, she leaned over to the table and asked in a low voice, "So why did you apologize for kissing me if you enjoyed it as much as I did?"

His bushy brow dipped into an I-don't-believe-you-asked-that frown, and she couldn't help but smile. Oh, for crying out loud. Hadn't he figured out by now that she was direct whenever she wanted to know something? It came with being Levy Michaels's daughter. At her house, with her secretive father, if she didn't ask she never knew what was going on.

"I didn't apologize for kissing you because I hadn't wanted to do it," he finally said. "I apologized for doing it because I have a rule never to mix business with pleasure."

A mischievous smile touched her lips. "And you consider me pleasure?"

He leaned back in his chair and stared at her while fingering his sexy beard. "What do you think?"

"I asked first," she countered, watching him. He was contemplating what he would say, and whatever it was, she wished he would get it out and stop sitting there, trying to tell her why he thought of her as pleasure when his gaze was pretty much voicing it for him.

Although she was taken by his perfect pair of lips, she also thought he had the most expressive eyes. She couldn't read him, as it was obvious he was keeping his inner feelings shielded. She recognized the tactic because she'd seen it in a lot of men and women who found shelter in her facilities. It wasn't that they had something to hide; it was that they had something they didn't want to share. And whatever it was served as a guard to keep people out.

To think that the successful Zion Blackstone could be grouped in that category was preposterous. Yet at Second Chances she'd seen it all. Anybody could have issues of some kind or another. Didn't she? That was why she'd named her charity Second Chances, so people would know that there was nothing wrong with starting over.

"It's not that complicated, Celine."

"Then why are you making it so? You don't mix business with pleasure—I get that. That means you see me as pleasure. Is it hard for you to admit it?"

He shrugged. "Why admit something you already know? Do you take perverse satisfaction in men admitting that you're beautiful, and that just looking at you gives them gratification?"

If he was trying to ruffle her feathers he was wasting her time. He didn't truly know her. If he did, then he would know she didn't have a conceited bone in her body. She was aware of the way the tabloids portrayed her, to sell papers. She didn't have the time or inclination to deny all the untruths they printed about her. However, she wouldn't pass up the chance to set him straight on a few things.

"First of all, I didn't call this meeting. You did. Secondly, if you have a problem kissing me, then keep your tongue inside your mouth. Thirdly, like any other woman, I like knowing men find me desirable. It's nothing to be ashamed about and I'm not. It's not like I set out to tease you, because I didn't. In fact, I don't recall doing anything to provoke that kiss. It just happened. That's the way of the world when there's sexual attraction between two individuals."

He took a sip of his water. She felt an ache at the juncture of her thighs while she watched his lips fit on the straw, and remembered the feel of them on her mouth.

Forcing her gaze off his lips, she said, "And fourthly, don't believe everything you read, especially when it involves me."

"Are you finished?"

"No, not yet. Fifthly, whatever issues you're dealing with, Zion, don't take it out on our kiss. A kiss that was so hot the thought of it still burns my lips."

She was grateful when, at that moment, the waiter returned with their food.

* * *

For crying out loud, did the woman say whatever she wanted? What right did she have to remind him how hot the kiss was? He, of all people, had been aware of all fifty degrees of pleasure. He'd felt the heat the moment he'd pulled her body against his and he'd breathed in her ever-arousing scent. The instant his tongue had entered her mouth and tangled with hers. She had returned the kiss as if it had been a long time since she'd been kissed by a man. Was that fact or wishful thinking on his part? Regardless, their mouths had mated in a way that still left him craving for more.

That in itself was so surreal that his body ached for her. Supposedly, they had gone to that escape room to have fun and work off nervous energy. He would admit to having fun, but he wasn't certain he'd worked off any energy. Nervous or otherwise. What he'd done was remember that because of his workload, he hadn't slept with a woman in months. That would be the first thing he remedied when he returned to Rome.

"If you don't dig in, your pizza will get cold."

Her words made him realize he was sitting there, staring at her like a demented fool. She was looking back at him with the intensity of a scientist studying the contents of a test tube.

Reaching out, he grabbed a slice of pizza, just as the waiter came to pour wine into their glasses. Good. He needed something stronger than water.

"I've said my piece, Zion. Now I want to give you time to speak yours," she said.

He wanted to ignore her, just savor the slice of pizza he'd bitten into. He now understood why she kept returning here. He loved pizza and this one was simply delicious. It was obvious the owner had used an old Italian recipe. There was nothing American about it.

Licking away some of the sauce that had dribbled on his lips, he glanced over and saw Celine watching him. The look he saw in her eyes nearly made him growl. Why was she staring so hard at his mouth? Was she remembering the kiss the same way he was? Recalling how it had started off slow and easy, but then ended up hard and demanding? Having memories of how their bodies molded together while their mouths greedily feasted off each other?

He hated admitting it, but he, a man who rarely lost control, had been unable to control himself with her. She affected him in a way he didn't understand, but he would fight tooth and nail to make sure such a thing didn't happen again.

"Are you going to help me finish off this pizza before it gets cold?" he asked her.

She smiled as she reached for another slice. "Doesn't matter to me. Cold or hot, I plan to eat it all. I take no prisoners."

He wondered what she did take, and was tempted to ask her. Given her penchant for directness, Zion knew she would probably tell him. She had definitely taken his kiss without any problem. Would she take his body into hers like it belonged there? Would she take kisses on that fine ass of hers like they belonged there, as well?

For Pete's sake, the thought of either of those scenarios had the lower part of his body throbbing. It was time he set her straight on a few things. He'd called for this meeting and now it was time to take ownership and make sure she understood his position.

"First of all, Celine, what I do have a problem with is mixing business with pleasure. I find you attractive but I don't intend to be distracted. I came here to get to know you, not to start anything I can't finish. I don't need to know you intimately to make jewelry to complement you.

Nor do I need to kiss you. Contrary to what you might think, I'm not taking anything out on our kiss. As much as I enjoyed it, I do regret it and I won't let it happen again. I'm not your type and you aren't mine, regardless of how much sexual chemistry we seem to generate."

When she didn't say anything, just stared at him, he decided to continue. "And I don't believe everything I read in the tabloids, since I've been the target of their sensationalism a few times myself."

"So, you see all the sexual chemistry flowing between us as wasted energy?" she asked, before biting into her pizza.

"Pretty much. So it will be up to us to keep a level head and make sure it doesn't consume us."

"Why should I?"

He lifted a brow. Was this her spoiled, I-can-have-anything-I-want attitude? Well, he had news for her. He had his own set of rules to follow and didn't intend to get sidetracked. Wasn't that how his mother had explained her one big mistake in life?

"The reason you should is because I refuse to be a willing partner," he said, trying not to show his annoyance. "I know what I came to Los Angeles to do and that's all I plan to do." In other words, he didn't intend to become any woman's sexual pastime, not even Celine's. No matter how badly he desired her, and he did desire her. What man wouldn't?

The waiter came to remove their empty plates and Zion appreciated the intrusion. The way she was sitting across the table, looking at him, it was as if his words had had no effect. The heated desire still on display in her eyes rattled every cell in his body. Damn.

A slow smile spread across her lips. "Are you ready, Zion?"

He swallowed deeply, unable to break eye contact with her. "For what?"

"To go. I'm sure you have a lot to do. I expect you'll be busy getting me those samples to look at before you leave, right? Unless you can think of something else you might want to do."

The mere suggestion ignited something deep within him. This woman was deadly. She was lethal. Headstrong. And oh, so damn sexy. She was a seductress if ever there was one. Celine Michaels, with her beautiful face, shapely body and sassy mouth, was trying to be his downfall. But he refused to let her. There was no doubt she was a handful.

Crap! Why had she chosen that moment to stretch her body by raising her arms above her head? The move made him notice her perfect-looking breasts and envision them in his hands before easing a nipple into his mouth.

"You never did answer my question, Zion."

He shifted his gaze from her chest to her face. "Your question?"

She chuckled, letting him know she'd been aware just where his attention had wandered. "Yes. Are you ready to go?"

"Yes," he said, standing and placing enough bills on the table to cover their meal and leave a very generous tip. Despite his protest, she had covered the cost of the escape room, but he wouldn't let her pay for lunch.

"I have a bad habit of wanting to have the last word, so I'm going to leave you with this prediction," she said, standing as well. She then leaned in close and whispered, "We will make love one day, Zion Blackstone, because it will be a waste of good sexual energy for us not to."

She then turned and walked out of the restaurant.

He watched her go and appreciated the sway of her ass with every sensual step she took. Drawing in a deep, frustrated breath, he felt fury build inside him, rippling to the same beat as his pulsating erection. Who the hell did she think she was, telling him what they would do, as if he had no say in the matter?

She was wrong. He had no intention of ever making love to Celine Michaels.

Chapter 6

Celine entered her bedroom, tossed her cross-body purse on the bed and shook her head at the thought of her audaciousness. What in the world had possessed her to say something like that to Zion? She'd outright told him they would make love one day, when she knew that wasn't true. She was not surprised that he hadn't spoken one single word to her on the way home. He wouldn't even look at her.

She was about to go into her connecting bath when her cell phone rang. Recognizing the ringtone, she quickly moved toward the bed to pull the cell phone from her purse. "Hey, Desha."

"I'm just checking to see how things went with Blackstone at the escape room."

Celine sat down on the side of the bed. "We had fun." She honestly thought they did. He'd seemed distant at first for some reason, but when he saw that advancing from room to room required them to work together to figure out the clues, he'd stopped being unapproachable. Only problem was that once he'd stopped acting detached, she couldn't stop noticing certain things about him. Why did he have to be one hundred degrees of fineness? No man should look that sexy in a pair of jeans and a polo shirt. Nor should he smell so darn good. And those times after they'd figured out a certain clue and he'd smiled, she'd wished a Zion Blackstone smile didn't always cause a sensuous shudder to pass through her.

And Lordy, she didn't want to think about the kiss, that smoking-hot kiss that had singed her brain cells and caused an indescribable ache between her thighs. As far as she was concerned, since he was the one to cause the ache, he should be the one to take it away. She knew only one way for him to do that, which was why she'd told him they would make love one day.

"Celine, you're still there?"

She was quickly reminded she had Desha on the phone. "Yes, I'm still here."

"Any reason you aren't focusing?"

Oh, she could think of only one reason. It was hard not to let her attention wander whenever she thought about a powerful, well-muscled body with broad shoulders, solid chest, flat abs, sinewy thighs and legs, and a too-handsome face. "Zion Blackstone is messing with my mind, Dee."

"Is he worth the nuisance?"

"That's debatable, although I did tell him that we'll be sleeping together one day."

She could hear her best friend's gasp. "You did what?"

"I know, I know. Doing something like that is so unlike me, right?"

"Being direct, no. Telling a man the two of you will be sleeping together, yes. What gives? I heard he's very handsome, but you've been around handsome men before. Lots of them. What makes him different?"

Now, that was a question she honestly couldn't answer. All she knew was that Zion had an effect on her. One she wished desperately he didn't have. She didn't think he was deliberately trying to seduce her or anything. In fact, she had a strong feeling that getting involved with her was the last thing he wanted. He had said as much.

Then why did you tell him that the two of you would be making love, like it was a foregone conclusion?

For some reason she liked pushing his buttons and seeing how far she could go. "Not sure what makes him different, but he is."

"And for you what does that mean, exactly?"

Desha had always been her voice of reason, her restorer of common sense and her calm before the storm. Could her best friend help her get through a potent case of sexual chemistry? "I'm not sure exactly what it means, other than I had no intention of being captivated by the likes of him. But…"

"But what?"

"Whenever he looks at me I feel things I've never felt before. And when we stand within a few feet of each other I actually can pick up his scent. *His* scent and not necessarily the cologne he's wearing. I always thought they were one and the same, but I found out they're not."

"Hmm, this is interesting."

A far as Celine was concerned, it was worse than interesting. It was crazy. "And he's not doing anything to encourage it."

"You sure about that?"

Celine thought about the kiss. "Positive. He seems somewhat annoyed by my interest."

"That's a first."

Celine fought back the twitch of a smile that threatened

her lips. Yes, it was. "I'm beginning to think that I'm losing it."

"Or maybe you're finally getting it."

"Meaning what?"

"Meaning that Zion Blackstone has placed you in a position you've never been in before."

Why did the word *position* suddenly conjure up a lot of naughty thoughts in her head? All sex positions. Him on top. Her on top. Her standing and pressed back against a shower wall. Her sitting spread-eagle on his lap… "Yes, you could definitely say that, Desha."

"Then you need to consider if you want to take this further. According to you, he'll be leaving tomorrow night."

"I don't want to take it further. I'm just going through a no-sex-in-a-long-time phase. After he leaves, he will be out of sight and out of mind."

"You're sure?" Desha asked, not sounding totally convinced.

"Positive." Celine hoped more than anything that was true.

"And what about Nikon?"

She rolled her eyes, wondering why Desha was even asking. "You know the deal with that, Desha. Nothing is going on between me and Nikon—it's all a publicity stunt. He and I haven't even kissed. Trust me when I say that Nikon does nothing for me."

"But Zion Blackstone does?"

Celine drew in a deep breath. "As much as I wish otherwise, yes, he does."

Zion leaned away from his laptop and smiled at the sketches of jewelry pieces he had designed. In his mind he could see Celine wearing them. For the necklace he had used a ruby partially enclosed in a three-quarter circle of diamonds shaped like the letter *C*, for *Celine*.

When dabbling around with ideas as to what style would work for her neck, he'd decided that although she wasn't a diamond girl, a few highlighting her ruby would be nice. Distinctive but not gaudy. Definitely laid-back but uniquely classy. He was also satisfied with images of the matching earrings.

Zion checked his watch, finding it hard to believe it was after midnight. Instead of going down to dinner he'd opted to remain in his room and concentrate on the designs. The kitchen staff had been kind enough to deliver a tray to his room and he'd appreciated it.

He'd called the airport to see if he could get an earlier flight back to Rome. If things worked out the way he hoped, he would fly out sooner. He was convinced Celine was trying to drive him crazy.

As busy as he needed to be, thoughts of her still managed to creep into his brain. That wasn't good at a time he needed to stay focused. She had to be the most desirable woman he'd met in a long time, and the most complicated. As soon as he thought he'd figured her out, she would do something that would make him scratch his head, or even worse, make his erection throb.

As soon as they'd arrived back at the Michaelses' home he hadn't wasted any time parting ways with her, saying he needed to get started on his designs. That hadn't exactly been a lie, but at the time it had been a necessity. Riding back in the car with her had been pure torture. Every time she'd shifted gears on that powerful little car of hers, his gaze had been drawn to how she gripped the stick shift and he imagined her gripping him the same way.

Working his neck to get the kinks out, he stood, deciding not to bother anyone from the kitchen to come get his tray. He could very well return it himself. Besides, he needed to stretch his legs.

Grabbing the tray off the table, he left his room. The house was quiet and he figured everyone had retired for the night.

Celine knew the moment Zion entered their overly large kitchen. It was so massive he hadn't seen her yet, but she'd seen him. This was where she would come as a kid when she wanted to sneak in and eat the dessert her father had forbidden her to have because she'd failed to eat her veggies at dinner.

"Looking for me, Zion?"

She knew he hadn't been, and the look of surprise on his features was better than priceless. It was comical at its best and pitiful at its worst. She was very much aware he'd skipped dinner because of her, evidently feeling the need to put distance between them.

"No, I'm not looking for you."

"Hmm, you don't sound convincing," she said, coming out of the shadows of the pantry.

"That's your take on things, not mine," he said, watching as she came closer.

His gaze was on her, all over her, and she sort of felt naked while fully clothed in a pair of shorts and a tank top. The gaze roving over her radiated heat that was a little too hot for her peace of mind at the moment. What was it with them and all this strong sexual chemistry that just wouldn't go away? Why did she find him so darn tempting? How was he able to stoke her fire without much effort? And why was he looking at her like she was a dessert he thought was bad for him, but wanted anyway?

She came to a stop in front of him. "I'm harmless, you know."

He lifted a brow. "Are you?"

"Yes, but…"

"And what's the *but*?"

"The *but* is that I'm only as harmless as you want me to be."

He chuckled and she felt him thawing a little, getting less uptight. She recalled him laughing and smiling a lot when they'd been in the escape room…before the kiss happened. A kiss she just couldn't forget.

"You're something else, you know."

She smiled. "I see that as a compliment, Zion. In fact, I refuse to see it as anything other than that."

He chuckled again and for some reason the sound made her feel all bubbly inside. "That's your prerogative, Celine."

She liked how he said her name, with a sort of Italian pitch to it. There was something about Zion she couldn't quite put her finger on. It wasn't anything he was deliberately trying to hide, but something she'd need to have a keen sense of observation to pick up on.

"I'll be leaving in the morning."

She lifted a brow, surprised. "In the morning? I thought you were leaving tomorrow night."

He shrugged. "I finished sooner than I thought I would. I'll email copies of the designs to your father and he'll share them with you. I'll be talking to him later in the week to get an approval to continue."

She nodded, noting that he was taking steps to ensure he wouldn't have to communicate directly with her anymore. "In that case, we can say our goodbyes now," she said, fighting to keep the disappointment out of her voice. "Goodbye, Zion. Have a safe flight back to Rome."

She moved to walk past him and he unexpectedly grabbed hold of her arm. The touch seemed to electrify every cell within her body. She looked up at him when he held on tightly. "Yes?"

Their gazes clashed. "It was nice meeting you, Celine."

She wasn't sure it had been nice meeting him. He had rattled her from the first and had reminded her how it felt to be a woman and how long it had been since she'd had sex with a man. The thought of the latter sent warm, sensuous vibes through her body. "Is that all you have to say, Zion?"

He continued to hold her gaze. Instead of answering her question, he asked one of his own. "Where are you going?"

She figured he'd asked because she was headed in the opposite direction from the doorway leading out of the kitchen. "Down to the wine cellar to grab a bottle. You can join me there if you like." At that moment, she knew what she wanted, and was tired of pretending. Was he?

He dropped his hand from her arm, and she figured apparently not, for he said, "I don't think that's a good idea."

She nodded. "Suit yourself." She then walked off.

Celine felt her breath wobble, knowing he was still standing there watching her leave. But what had she expected? He'd made it clear that he didn't mix business with pleasure.

Pressing the button for the elevator, she was tempted to glance back at him, but refused to do so. Even when she stepped onto the elevator she kept her back to him until the door swooshed shut behind her. That was when she turned around and released the breath she'd been holding.

When the elevator door opened to the wine cellar, she stepped out into the huge climate-controlled storage room, where thousands of bottles of wine were stored. She'd always thought this was a beautiful place, with the stone walls and detailed lighting fixtures on the ceiling.

The wine cellar had been designed by her father. Years ago it had been his private sanctuary whenever he needed his full concentration to study the script for his next movie. It had also been the place he would bring his friends for private conversations, which was why a huge conference table was placed in one section of the room, along with a bar and several stools.

She was about to head toward the rack where her favorite wine was kept when the elevator door opened and Zion walked out. Her gaze drifted over him and she could feel an urgency sizzle within her at the way he was looking at her.

"I decided to accept the invitation to join you," he said, coming closer. "And you know what else I've decided to do?"

She swallowed deeply. "No. What?"

"To once again break one of my rules."

Chapter 7

Celine drew in a deep breath, wondering exactly what that meant. Did he plan to kiss her like he had at the escape room, or was he thinking about doing more? Her body had begun responding the moment she saw him walk off that elevator and it was still responding. She was getting aroused by everything that was Zion Blackstone. His looks, his dress and even the way he smelled. It was weird how her erogenous zones were igniting and he had yet to touch her.

When he came to a stop in front of her she had to tilt her head back to stare up into his dark eyes. "Break another rule? Do you think that's wise?"

Her stomach tightened at the way his mouth eased into a smile. "After deliberately pushing all my buttons, Celine, are you now trying to talk me out of anything?"

Was she? Frankly, she wasn't sure what he had in mind. Did it matter? All she knew was that it was close to two in the morning, and they were alone in the cellar, surrounded by thousands of bottles of wine and encased in sexual chemistry.

"Well, are you?"

She shook her head. "No, I'm not trying to talk you out of anything."

He nodded. "Now that we have that cleared up…"

Zion reached out and touched her arms, and she pulled in a sharp breath when a sensuous shiver flowed through her. It was as if every hormone in her body was suddenly sizzling. No other man had ever made her feel the things Zion was.

"What you said about this sexual chemistry between us was right," Zion said, in a deep, throaty voice. "There is too much of it between us to waste."

A spike of heat hit her dead center at the juncture of her legs. "So, what do you plan to do with it?"

"For starters, this."

He pulled her to him, lowered his head and kissed her. The moment their mouths connected, a tiny moan broke past her lips, only to be captured by his mouth as it devoured hers with a hunger she had not been prepared for. A hunger she felt all the way to her toes.

Instinctively, she pressed her body closer, and when she felt his hard erection against her, she knew it was solid evidence of his desire for her. Would he settle for just this kiss? Would he want to do more to kindle the passion between them? Did she want him to? They had met only yesterday. Weren't they moving a little too fast?

Too late to consider that now. She was consumed by something so delicious, the last thing she wanted was for him to stop kissing her. She loved the feel of his tongue in her mouth, loved the erotic movements that were causing all sorts of sensations to flood her nervous system. She was convinced no man's tongue should be able to do the things to her that his was doing. It was giving her pleasure to a degree she didn't think was possible from a simple kiss.

And then suddenly, he pulled his mouth away, leaving her breathing hard.

Zion stared down at Celine. What was there about her that made him want her so badly? The intensity of the kiss they'd just shared had shaken him to the core, had given him the purest pleasure a man could get while inside a woman's mouth. It tempted him to get inside her body, as well.

Damn, at that moment he didn't just want her—he needed her. And he resented it, because he had never needed any woman. He refused to need one. No woman would ever become so essential that he'd break any of the rules he'd made. Yet here he was, doing that very thing.

He knew he should be fighting temptation with everything within him, but was unable to do it. Instead, he reached out and curved a hand to her neck, bringing her mouth back to his, needing to kiss her again.

Zion wanted her and consequences be damned. He was about to undress her when he suddenly realized he'd left his wallet upstairs. Inside that wallet was the condom he needed. That realization was like ice water being poured on him and he suddenly broke off their kiss.

"Zion?"

He looked down at her and saw how wet her lips were. Wet from how he'd made love to her mouth. Knowing he should be feeling thankful rather than frustrated, he drew in a deep breath and took a step back. He inwardly fought to reclaim control of his senses while ignoring the throbbing ache behind his zipper. He'd wanted her. He still wanted her. But deep down he knew having her would be a mistake.

He broke eye contact with her and hung his head as if deep in thought. He couldn't think straight, looking at her. When he glanced up again the gaze that met his was so intense that he knew she wanted him as much as he wanted her.

Considering the circumstances, he knew the only way their time together could end. He took a step closer to her, leaned down and brushed his lips against hers, feeling a sense of loss all the way to his toes. "Goodbye, Celine."

He saw something—he wasn't sure what—flash in her eyes before she said, "Goodbye, Zion."

He turned and was headed to the elevator when she called out to him. "Zion?"

He slowly turned around and met her gaze, bracing himself for what she would say. "Yes?"

"Thanks for breaking your rule again tonight. I needed it."

He was tempted to cross the room, sweep her into his arms, carry her over to that table and take her long and hard on it. Instead he said, "I needed it, as well."

Then he turned and, forcing his legs to move, continued toward the elevator.

Chapter 8

Rome, Italy, a month later

"Are you sure you're okay, son?"

Zion took another sip of his coffee as he spoke into his cell phone. "I'm fine, Pop. You worry too much."

"Well, what am I supposed to do when I hear you're not coming home for the holidays?"

"That's not definite," Zion said, dropping his head back against the sofa, although he knew in a way that it was. "I might surprise everyone."

"I hope you do. I think your godbrothers think you prefer not being around them now that they're married and you're not. I wished the six of you hadn't formed that darn club."

Zion chuckled. "They know better than that, and the club has nothing to do with it. I am happy for them and their wives are the best."

"Well, if that's not what's keeping you away, then what is, Zion? Why don't you like coming home?"

Zion rubbed a hand down his face and wished he could tell his dad what had bothered him for close to nine years. If he were to ever reveal his mother's deathbed confession it would probably destroy his father. "You're imagining things. I do like coming home."

"You could have fooled me. In fact, I never knew why you wanted to leave the United States and live so far away right after your mother died. I know losing Alyse was hard on you, but it was hard on me, too."

Zion hung his head and closed his eyes for a second. He knew how hard it had been for his father to lose the woman he'd met and fallen in love with. Of the six close friends from Morehouse, his father had been the last to marry, claiming he'd been in no hurry to end his bachelor days. Pretty much how Zion felt now. His parents had met when his businessman father had gotten hurt on a ski trip with friends, and was taken to the emergency room where Zion's mother was on duty as a nurse.

"I know, Dad. I know how much you loved Mom." He opened his eyes, thinking, *Too bad she didn't love you as much.*

"It was nine years last week, son. It's hard to believe, isn't it?"

Zion lifted his head. "Yes, it's hard to believe." All of it. He could remember it just like it was yesterday. He often wondered why he had to find out when his mother was dying that she'd been unfaithful to the man who'd loved her. A man who was determined to keep her memory alive.

"I went to the cemetery to place flowers on her grave."

Zion didn't say anything. He truly didn't have to. Langren Blackstone had slipped into that melancholy mood. It always happened this time every year, around the anniversary of his wife's death.

"Pop?"

"Yes?"

"Have you given any thought to dating? Look at Goddaddy Anthony. He seems happy with Claire. None of us thought he'd ever get over Carolyn."

Anthony Lassiter, Uriel's father, had married Claire Steele a few months ago. About five years before, Anthony's first wife of over thirty years, Uriel's mother, had asked for a divorce so she could date younger men. The divorce had left Anthony in a bad way emotionally. He and Claire had dated for almost three years before deciding to make their relationship permanent. That meant a second chance at love was possible for some people.

"Anthony *is* happy with Claire and I'm happy for him. Things are different with me. I doubt that I can ever love another woman beside your mother. There can be only one woman for me."

Zion tightened his jaw to refrain from saying it was too bad his mother hadn't thought there could be only one man for her. He hung his head again, knowing his father would never learn that the wife he loved endlessly had betrayed him.

"I might surprise you and come home. I won't say when," Zion said to his father.

"That would be nice if you did."

"How's your golf game coming along?" he asked, knowing it was time to change the subject. For the next ten minutes Zion listened to his father. When they finally ended the call, he stood and stretched.

More than once he had come close to telling his dad the truth of what his mother had done, but Zion knew he never would. All it took was for him to remember how emotionally damaged his godfather Anthony had been after finding out his wife hadn't been the woman he thought she was for all those years. Zion refused to let his father go through that.

His mother's infidelity, although she'd sworn to Zion it had happened only once, was one of the reasons he'd moved to Rome not long after her death. It had been hard seeing his father stricken with grief for a wife who hadn't been faithful to him. And Zion being privy to her indiscretion made him feel guilty and as much of a traitor as his mother had been.

It was Zion's secret, one he'd shared only with his godbrothers. The guys felt whether he was Langren Blackstone's biological son would be an easy enough thing to prove or disprove just by checking their DNA, but Zion didn't want to risk his father ever finding out that the woman he'd loved so much had once been unfaithful to him. So instead of hanging around and letting something slip, Zion had moved to Rome.

Easing back on the sofa, he grabbed the TV remote, deciding to see what was on the American stations he was able to get. He was flipping through the various channels when something being said on *Entertainment News* caught his attention. "What the hell?" He sat up straight to hear what the announcer was saying.

"According to Nikon Anastas, he has asked Celine Michaels to marry him and she's accepted. No details of when the happy couple will be tying the knot, but we'll keep you abreast of those details later..."

A photo of Celine and Anastas in a happy embrace flashed across the screen. Zion clicked off the remote and the television went black. He tried to control emotions he didn't want to feel, had no right to feel. He went to the kitchen for a beer.

Celine Michaels. The woman with whom he'd shared a blazing sexual chemistry that even now, a month later, made him think about her constantly.

He'd been convinced that there had been something powerful, dynamic and monumental going on between them. There had to have been for him to react to her the way he had back then.

And now, barely a month later, she was getting married.

He twisted the cap off his beer bottle and took a huge swig. She had asked him if he was seriously involved with anyone, but he hadn't asked her. He'd just assumed she wasn't. But if she was getting married, that meant she and the guy must have been involved when she had let Zion kiss her. Down in that wine cellar, he'd come within seconds of making love to her. How could a woman commit to one man and let another man take liberties with her that way?

Wasn't that the same question he had asked his mother?

He took another long swig of his beer and finished it off. Anger began consuming him and he felt like throwing the bottle against the wall. But he refused to let another woman break him down.

Celine's plane had landed in Rome yesterday and she was convinced if she had to attend another party she was going to scream. The nerve of her father, bailing out at the last minute and not flying to Europe with her. Especially since coming here had been his idea, not hers.

And then to make matters worse, Desha had called a few hours ago to give her a heads-up that the media were claiming she and Nikon had gotten engaged, and that Nikon himself had made the announcement. What kind of foolishness was that? She had tried calling him, but his press secretary said he wasn't available and she'd give him the message Celine had phoned. So far she hadn't heard from him.

She had been able to reach her father, who assured her that what had gotten leaked to the press was nothing more than a PR move and that he would explain everything in detail when she returned to the States. It angered her that he felt he could make such a move without her permission. She had given him fair warning that if she got accosted by the paparazzi in Rome, she would tell them Nikon was the last man she would marry. Her father had tried talking her out of it, saying it would ruin an extensive PR strategy he and Nikon had concocted, but she didn't care.

Her father's actions were just more proof that it was time for her to stop allowing him to manipulate and control her. It was time she made some important decisions in her life. When she returned home she would tell him she intended to move out. Then she would tell him about her involvement with Second Chances. Lastly, she would let him know her life was no longer his to control and manipulate.

Settling in the back seat of the limo, she glanced out the window and marveled at the beautiful architectural designs of the buildings they passed. She wished the picturesque views of Rome could stop her mind from wandering, but they couldn't.

The moment the plane had landed, the first thought that had entered her mind was that this was where Zion lived. Zion Blackstone, the one man she just couldn't seem to forget. There hadn't been a single day during the past thirty that she hadn't thought of him.

She should have known from the first time she'd laid eyes on him, from the intensity of his gaze as he'd stared back at her, that he would be someone she wouldn't easily forget. She thought she could ignore him, but that hadn't worked. The sexual tension between them seemed only to escalate. And suggesting they go to the escape room hadn't been a bright idea, after all. Just being around him had sensitized every sensuous nerve in her body, reminded her that she had hormones that could rear up at times, and made her pulse race at an alarming speed.

It was there that he'd pulled her to him and kissed her in a way that had totally and thoroughly messed up her mind. She had figured nothing could have been that good, but here it was a month later and she had to concede that it truly had been.

He had seduced her. Not with words but with action, the way he'd given her a full-contact, hot and heavy, wet-tongue, tonsil-touching kiss. And he was seducing her mind, sight unseen, with memories. At times they were so vivid she had to take a deep breath to stop her pulse from escalating.

When the private car rolled up to the huge mansion, she instructed the driver in Italian not to leave, because she intended to stay less than thirty minutes. That would give her a chance to make an appearance and say hello to the American ambassador and his lovely wife. Then she would go back to the hotel, and pack to return to the States first thing in the morning.

Several Italian reporters tried getting a statement from her as she hurried up the steps to the party. She ignored them and kept going, and was glad when the guards forced them back.

Celine remained at the party for a little while and was about to leave when a tall man approached. "Ms. Michaels, I'm Stefano Calabria, assistant to the ambassador," he said, flashing his credentials and speaking with a deep Italian accent. "Word has reached the ambassador that the paparazzi are out front. He's instructed me to handle the matter. I've requested that your driver bring your car around back. Please follow me."

"All right." She followed the man, grateful the ambassador had the insight to assist her in avoiding the paparazzi.

The car was waiting and Mr. Calabria opened the door.

"Thanks," she said, smiling up at the man as she slid onto the smooth leather seat.

"You're welcome, *signorina*. Enjoy the rest of your evening."

The car moved away and she settled back against her seat. Moments later she noticed they were taking a different route than the one they'd used earlier. "Any reason we're going a different way?" she asked the driver.

"No reason, *signorina*."

She frowned, suddenly noting this was not the same man. "Wait a minute. You aren't my driver. Who are you and where is he?"

The man chuckled. "He's indisposed at the moment. Just relax. We're in for a long ride."

A long ride? The hotel where she was staying was only ten minutes away. Where was this guy taking her? "Where are we going?"

"Not sure what your end destination will be. I was told to take you to a place several miles from here to wait for further orders."

To wait for orders? What on earth was going on? "Your orders from whom?"

"Please, *signorina*. No more questions. Just sit back and enjoy the ride."

Like hell she would. "You will tell me what I want to know and you will tell me now," she said, with forcefulness in her voice.

The vehicle came to a traffic light and the driver turned around in his seat to stare back at her. He removed his chauffeur cap and tossed it on the seat beside him. "Your fiancé owes us money. He's promised to pay within a week. And you, Miss Michaels, are our collateral until he does. That means you will be our guest. And just in case you're tempted to try using your mobile phone, we've blocked all incoming and outgoing calls."

Celine stared at the man, certain she'd misunderstood him. But seeing the serious look on his face, she knew she had not. "First of all, I don't have a fiancé. Secondly, I am an American citizen and you can't block my calls or hold me against my will. And—"

"Unfortunately, you have no say in the matter. And you are Nikon Anastas's fiancée. It was announced in the media that you are and he verified as much to us."

"Well, it's not true, and I want to be taken to the hotel now."

The traffic light changed and the vehicle continued…in the wrong direction. She knew what he'd said, but pulled her phone out of her purse anyway. When she clicked it on, the words *Not in Service* flashed across the screen. She glared at the driver. "You can't hold me against my will."

"You've said that already. And just so you know, Anastas knows you're being held until he pays up. He has no problem with our arrangement and says he will come get you in a week."

"A week? If I go missing for a week without a trace, my father will contact the American embassy for answers."

"Anastas assured us that won't happen, and from what I heard, your old man is aware of Anastas's plan."

Celine sat up in her seat. Her father? What was this man talking about? There was no way her father would go along with this. "I don't believe you. My dad would never do anything to place my life in danger."

The man laughed. "I didn't say he would. I think Nikon convinced him your life wouldn't be in danger, and it won't. Just as long as Nikon comes through for us by paying the debt he owes, you'll be all right."

Celine didn't say anything. She was too busy thinking

of how she would get out of this. She was boiling mad. How dare her father and Nikon involve her in something like this. "Look, mister, you can't keep me here against my will."

"Your fiancé said we can."

"I keep telling you I don't have a fiancé. I will have you arrested for kidnapping."

"It's not kidnapping, *signorina*. It's safekeeping. Your accommodations will be excellent and we have been instructed to see to your every whim."

When he pulled the vehicle into the parking lot of what looked like a market, he said, "I smoked my last cigarette and will go into this all-night store to grab a pack. Don't waste your time trying to get out because you're locked in."

Celine knew now might be her only chance to get away. She couldn't go back to the hotel, since that was the first place they would look for her. And she couldn't go to the police until she knew how her father was involved. "Wait! I need to use the ladies' room," she said, when he opened the door to get out.

"No. We will reach our destination in less than an hour."

"I can't wait that long. For goodness' sake, what can a helpless woman like me do?"

The man glared at her for a moment, and then, as if he agreed with the assessment of her weakness, he said, "I will walk you to the ladies' room and wait for you to come out. Don't try anything crazy while you are in there."

She didn't intend to make it to the restroom. She had scoped out the area and they were still close to downtown Rome. She didn't know how many people were involved in this. So far she knew of the guy who'd identified himself as the ambassador's assistant at the party and this driver. Were there others? Those involved would be looking for her, and she quickly thought of where she could go and hide out.

"Remember what I said. No funny business," he repeated, opening the door for her.

As soon as she was out of the car, she turned on him and did what her friends, the Moretti triplets, had told her to do if she was ever in such a situation. She gave the man a hard kick below the belt. He went down and she took off running.

Chapter 9

Zion was awakened from a sound sleep by the buzzing of his security intercom system. Well, not exactly a sound sleep, not when he was in the throes of a hot dream. In a way, he appreciated the intrusion. He had no business dreaming about Celine Michaels, anyway. She was now an engaged woman.

He wondered why Parker was buzzing him. It was close to two in the morning. No one would be visiting him at this hour. He reached for his cell phone and pressed the single digit that connected him with the head of his security. "Yes, Parker?" he asked in a sluggish voice. "What is it?"

"Mr. Blackstone, I hate to bother you, but there's a woman here requesting to see you."

Zion rolled his eyes. The last thing he wanted was to be bothered by some woman intent on making a booty call. Hmm, then maybe not. He'd seriously thought about hooking up with someone since returning from California, but the thought of having sex with anyone other than Celine

Michaels had been a turnoff. Not anymore. The sooner he could bed some other woman, the better. Then maybe he could stop having dreams about Celine.

"What's her name?"

"She won't give me a name, sir. She said to tell you 'Bye, Felicia,' and you would know who she was."

Bye, Felicia? Zion jerked upright in bed. It couldn't be. Why would the very woman he'd just been dreaming about show up at his place at two in the morning? And wasn't she engaged to marry that Anastas guy? So what was she doing coming here? "Put her on the phone."

"Yes, sir." He could hear Parker handing her the phone. "Zion?"

"What are you doing here, Celine?"

"I'll explain everything to you when I see you."

Not a chance, he thought. There was no way in hell he would invite her up to his place. Besides, there was nothing for her to explain. "Don't waste your breath explaining anything to me. Those kisses we shared meant nothing."

"Thanks for letting me know that, but that's not why I'm here."

"Then why are you here at two in the morning?"

"I need help, Zion, and I didn't know of anyone else I could go to."

He rolled his eyes. "And just what sort of help do you need?"

She didn't say anything for a minute, and then whispered, so low he could barely hear her, "Someone tried to kidnap me tonight."

Had he heard her right? "Someone tried to kidnap you?"

"Yes, but I managed to get away. He's probably out there looking for me. You have to help me, Zion."

He rubbed his hand down his face. Honestly, was he supposed to believe this crazy story? But what if she was telling the truth? He couldn't imagine her making up something like that. If she was telling the truth, then why was she here and not at police headquarters or at the American embassy?

As if she knew what he was thinking, she said, "I am telling you the truth, Zion. Otherwise, I wouldn't be here."

Releasing a deep breath, he said, "Put Parker back on the line."

Seconds later, Parker returned. "Yes, sir?"

"Send her up."

The moment Celine stepped off the elevator she saw Zion standing there, leaning his broad shoulders in an open door frame. He wore nothing but PJ bottoms with a drawstring at the waist, hung low on his hips. The lighting from the corridor ceiling illuminated his bare chest, all muscle and sinew. And those dreadlocks that flowed over his shoulders made him appear wild, untamed, definitely edgier than he'd looked in Los Angeles.

Her knees seemed to give out on her with every step she took. But then, it could have been from sheer exhaustion. She had run several blocks in heels before finally taking them off. Once she'd reached the area where Zion lived, she felt a bit more comfortable, since she knew her way around.

The closer she got to him, the more she resented that the chemistry was still there between them. The way he was looking at her was stirring all kinds of sensations within her. Sensations she'd rather not deal with right now. She had enough problems on her hands.

She noticed when concern abruptly had replaced the expression on his face. Evidently, he could see that her sleeve was ripped and that she was limping. She figured she looked a mess.

Zion straightened. "You okay?" he asked, and she could hear actual worry in his voice.

She nodded as she came to a stop in front of him. "Yes, I'm okay."

He stood aside for her to enter his home. She glanced around and saw how huge and immaculate his place was.

"Okay, Celine, what the hell happened?"

She turned to him. Instead of answering him, she asked, "May I have something to drink? Something strong?"

He looked at her for a moment, before nodding. "Follow me." She trailed behind him to his kitchen. "Go ahead and have a seat."

She was grateful to finally get off her feet, and sat at the table. Glancing around, she saw his kitchen was just as immaculate as the rest of the rooms she'd seen so far. "Thanks."

He opened his cabinet and retrieved what looked like a bottle of scotch and two glasses, and placed them on the table in front of her. She'd been right. It was scotch, and he poured a generous amount into one of the glasses.

She held his gaze as she took a sip, then closed her eyes when the liquor burned her throat. She was a wine drinker, but tonight she needed something stronger, and this scotch certainly did the trick.

"Now you want to tell me what happened?" he asked, taking a seat at the table.

No, she didn't want to tell him, but since she'd shown up at his place at two in the morning, he deserved an explanation. "I was invited to a party given by the American ambassador. It was held at one of the ballrooms at the Circus Maximus." She figured he was familiar with the place, since it was an ancient Roman chariot-racing stadium and mass entertainment venue in Rome. The most lavish parties were often held there.

"And?"

"And when I was leaving, a man who introduced himself as an assistant to the ambassador told me that because there were paparazzi out front, he'd ordered my limo to be brought to the back."

"And you believed this man?"

"Yes, I had no reason not to believe him. He'd flashed his credentials in front of me. I should have taken the time to look at them carefully, but I didn't." Now she wished she had.

"It was only after I noticed that the driver was going in a different direction that I questioned him about it. That's when I realized it was not the same driver who'd taken me to the event. He told me that Nikon Anastas owed someone a large amount of money and that I was being held as collateral until it was paid in a week. But what really pissed me off was that this man claimed Nikon was very much aware I was going to be held."

Zion's brow arched. "Your fiancé was willing to use you that way?"

She frowned. "First of all, Nikon is not my fiancé."

"He's not your fiancé *now*?"

"He's never been my fiancé."

Zion shrugged. "That's not what I heard on television earlier."

"Evidently, you and a number of others. Whatever you heard is a lie."

Zion leaned back in his chair. "And why would Anastas lie about something like that?"

"I have no idea. I couldn't convince the guy who was driving that car tonight that Nikon wasn't my fiancé."

Zion didn't say anything while she took another sip of scotch. Then he asked, "So, how did you get away from this kidnapper?"

"He stopped to run into this place for a pack of cigarettes, and I convinced him I needed to use the bathroom. When he opened the door, I kicked him hard in the groin and he went down on his knees and I took off."

Zion didn't say anything as he filled his own glass with scotch. He took a sip. Then he held her gaze when he asked, "So, why did you come here and not go to the police or the embassy and report what happened? Kidnapping is a serious offense. Besides, you're an American citizen."

"Yes, but…"

She went silent. How was she going to tell him that according to the driver, her father had known about it? She hoped that was a lie Nikon had told, just like he'd put out that lie that she was his fiancée. But what if the man had told the truth and Nikon had talked her father into something so outlandish? If she was to report anything to the authorities, that could get her father in serious trouble. She didn't care one iota about Nikon, but her father was a different matter.

"But what, Celine?"

She nervously nibbled on her bottom lip. How could she make such a bizarre charge against her father? But still, Zion deserved to know why she hadn't gone to the authorities. "The man also made some claims against someone else. He claimed this person knew about the kidnapping, as well."

She saw how Zion's jaw tightened. Although he was holding it in check, she saw anger in the dark eyes staring at her. "Who?"

She drew in a slow breath before saying, "My father."

"You honestly believe that?" Zion asked, when his shock subsided. What man would be involved in kidnapping his own child? For her to even reveal something like that meant there was a possibility Levy Michaels was capable of such a thing.

She took another sip, then pushed the glass away. "I truly don't know what to believe, Zion. I don't want to believe it, but Dad has been acting pretty strange lately."

"In what way?"

"Well, for starters, when I first got wind of Nikon's claim of our engagement, I called my father when I couldn't reach Nikon. Dad all but told me to just go along with the lie because it was nothing more than a publicity stunt. That's how he got me to start dating Nikon in the beginning. When I told him I wouldn't do any such thing, that this farce of a relationship had gone too far and that Nikon had crossed the line with his recent claim of our engagement, Dad pleaded with me to go along with it and told me that it would all be over in a week or so."

"What did he mean by that?" Zion asked.

"I have no idea."

"Why didn't you call your father once you got away from the kidnappers?"

"I would have called Dad, but my phone was blocked." She reached into her purse, pulled out her phone and handed it to him. "See? No service," she said, after clicking it on. "It worked fine up until I left the party tonight."

Zion took the phone from her, fighting to ignore the sensations that swept through him when their hands touched. When he heard her sharp intake of breath, he knew she'd felt it, as well. That stimulated sexual chemistry that had captivated them before was still there. If anything, it seemed stronger than ever.

He studied her phone. She was right; it had gotten blocked of all incoming and outgoing calls. "You could use mine to call him."

"But then he'll know I'm with you. If he's somehow involved in this, I prefer he not know where I am."

Zion nodded, thinking that made sense. "Then I have the perfect solution," he said, getting up from the table. "I'll be right back."

Celine watched Zion leave the kitchen, wondering what his perfect solution was. She then wondered about all that heated desire that sizzled her insides each and every time he looked at her. Coming here might not have been a good idea, but she couldn't think of anywhere else to go. She would have gone straight to the airport if she hadn't left her passport in her hotel room.

She took a deep breath, refusing to drink any more scotch. She just couldn't understand how Zion always ignited sparks of sexual excitement within her the way he did. When she'd watched him leave the kitchen, she thought even his walk was sinfully erotic.

She glanced at her watch. It was nearly two in the morning, which meant it was close to five o'clock in the afternoon in Los Angeles. Had Nikon been notified she'd gotten away? Was her father aware of it, as well?

"Here. You can use this," Zion said, returning and handing her a cell phone. "It's a burner and can't be traced back to me." She noticed he had changed out of his PJ bottoms into a pair of jeans, but hadn't bothered to put on a shirt.

She stared down at what he'd given her. There was no need to ask why he had a burner phone. Desha's brother, Jordan, had one, as well, and had explained it was the number he gave to women he didn't want having his actual mobile number. Jordan called it his booty-call phone. Did Zion use this phone for the same purpose? And why did it bother her if he did?

"Thanks." She took it and immediately placed a call

to her father. She put the phone on speaker so Zion could listen in.

"Hello?"

"Dad, this is Celine."

"Celine! Where are you?"

She glanced over at Zion and knew he was thinking the same thing she was. For her father to ask her whereabouts meant he knew she was not in place. "And just where am I supposed to be, Dad?"

"Stop playing games with me. I've been worried sick about you."

"Oh, you are worried sick about me? Really? Is that why you went along with some crazy scheme Nikon concocted to have me kidnapped until he satisfied his debt to a bunch of goons?"

"Is that what you believe?"

"That's what I was told, and the man telling the story sounded pretty convincing. I don't know what Nikon has gotten himself into, but for you to agree and put me in danger is unacceptable and unforgivable."

"You were never in danger, Celine. Nikon assured me that you wouldn't be."

"And you believed him?"

"I saw no reason not to, since he's your fiancé."

Celine saw red. "Nikon is *not* my fiancé and you know it! The only reason I was dating him was because you asked me to. But now both you and Nikon have crossed the line. Tonight I was kidnapped, Dad. Do you hear me? I was kidnapped. I was being held until Nikon paid off his debt, and these men weren't lightweights. They were professionals. And honestly, I don't feel safe going to the authorities here."

"Please don't go to the authorities, Celine. Just be at the airport in the morning. I will send Ulysses with the jet for you." Ulysses was her father's personal pilot.

"Don't bother. Right now I'm having a problem believing those men won't be at the airport instead of Ulysses. I won't take that chance."

"Where are you?"

"I'm not saying. I can't believe it's come to this, but I can't trust you right now, Dad. I don't know why you went along with Nikon and why you put your only daughter's life in danger."

"I told you. Your life was never in danger and I am not mixed up in anything. If you won't tell me where you are, will you at least assure me that you're safe?"

"I am safe for now." She regretted she couldn't be more forthcoming with him than that.

"I still wish you would come home. Even if you don't want Ulysses to come for you, book your own flight and come home."

"Right now I don't feel safe doing that, either. Bye, Dad." She clicked off the phone and handed it back to Zion.

Drawing in a deep breath, she said, "If I can crash on your sofa tonight, I promise to leave first thing in the morning."

"And go where?"

She shrugged. "Not sure yet. I wish I could get my things from the hotel, but I'm too afraid to go back there."

"What hotel were you staying at?"

"The Inspiron."

He nodded. "Don't worry about sleeping on the sofa. I have guest rooms, and tonight, Celine Michaels, you are my houseguest."

Chapter 10

"Thanks, Alessandro. I owe you one," Zion said to the friend he was talking to on his cell phone.

"No problem, Zion. I'll take Isabella with me to pack up everything. I don't feel comfortable touching all that feminine stuff."

Zion rolled his eyes. Isabella was Alessandro Rossi's younger sister. "Whatever. Just be careful. There's a chance the place is being watched."

Alessandro chuckled. "Have you forgotten that cautious is my middle name? I should be at your place before breakfast time."

Zion checked the clock on the wall. It was almost four in the morning now. "Okay. I'll see you then."

He clicked off the phone and sighed deeply. It was a stroke of luck that Alessandro's family owned the Inspiron Hotel, and he figured Celine would be happy to get her things back. He had loaned her one of his T-shirts to sleep in tonight and had told her about the toiletry kits in each vanity.

Zion could hear the shower going, which meant she was getting ready for bed. After her ordeal tonight, he figured she would be both mentally and physically drained. He could only wonder what in the world Nikon Anastas was involved in. And although Levy Michaels tried convincing his daughter otherwise, Zion wasn't sure her father could be trusted, either. What man would go along with something so crazy? But then, to give the man credit, it sounded as if Nikon had outright lied to Michaels as to what was going down. Why? And just what *was* going down? After listening to that conversation between Celine and her father, Zion couldn't help but be curious. And why did knowing she was not an engaged woman, had never been one, make him feel good inside?

He stretched, deciding that, in all reality, none of it was his business. In fact, he appreciated that Celine did not involve him by letting her father know she was at his place. There was no reason for Levy Michaels to think Celine would seek shelter with him. In the morning, once she got her luggage, she could be on her merry little way and his life could get back to normal. Right now, it was anything but that.

For starters, just listening to the sound of the water running for her shower was making him do crazy things. Like standing in his living room envisioning her naked. He wanted her. God, he wanted her, and the way his body was throbbing below the waist was letting him know how much. The sooner she left, the better. He would give her a place to stay tonight, but that was all she would get from him.

But, boy, would he like to give her more. Like the feel

of him sliding inside her. The feel of him thrusting in and out of her. The feel of—

"Oops. I didn't know you were still up."

He glanced over at Celine, realizing he hadn't heard the shower stop. She was standing in the hallway that led from the guest room, wearing his T-shirt, a black custom design with the words *By Zion* sprawled across the front in huge, bold white letters that stretched across her breasts. The shirt hit her midway down her curvy thighs and highlighted a pair of gorgeous legs. She looked too damn sexy for her good or his.

"Yes, I'm still up." *In more ways than one*, he thought, feeling his hard erection throb against the zipper of his jeans. "I wanted to make sure you were all settled in before I go back to bed."

"Thanks. I'm fine. I was just getting something to drink."

He nodded. "More scotch?"

She grinned at him. Why did she do that? Seeing a smile on her face for the first time tonight did something to him. "No. I'll pass on more scotch. I think I've had enough. Any more and I might oversleep, and I don't want to do that. I've caused you enough trouble already by being here. Sorry I interrupted your sleep."

Little did she know she had interrupted his sleep anyway, with all those dreams he'd been having of her since returning from the States. "So, what did you plan to drink?"

"Water."

"In that case, I have plenty. Help yourself."

He figured she had no idea how intoxicating her scent was. He had a feeling that even after she left it would linger for a couple of days.

"Thanks."

She walked off and his gaze followed her, not missing

how his shirt fit her backside. Desire escalated through him. It was time for him to call it a night before he did something stupid. Like follow her into the kitchen and cop a taste of her lips. She'd been through enough tonight and didn't need him to add any more problems to those she was dealing with now.

"I'll see you in the morning," he called out.

"All right. What time do you want me up and out?"

"No rush." He decided not to tell her chances were he would have her luggage before she woke up. He wanted to surprise her. "Good night."

"Good night, Zion. Oh, yeah, there is something I need to ask you about, though."

He left the living room and walked into the kitchen. She was leaning against the sink with a glass of water in her hand. Her stance looked too damn sexy for his peace of mind. "What do you want to ask me?"

"Do all your towels have your name monogrammed on them?"

He chuckled. "Just about. I like declaring ownership whenever I can."

"Do you?"

"Yes." Why had he said that? He could have just told her the simple truth. For the last five years, one of his godmothers, who owned a specialty shop in Seattle, had given each of her godsons personalized towel sets for Christmas. He expected the same this year.

"That's good to know."

"What is?"

"You and that ownership thing."

That ownership thing. He could just imagine her drying her naked body off with a towel with his name written on it. Like the T-shirt she was wearing. She was standing there staring at him in a way that charged his libido with enough sexual energy to last for days, months and even years. He couldn't help but wonder what she did have or didn't have on under his T-shirt. His fingertips tingled, and he was tempted to cross the room, skim them across her breasts while tracing the words *By Zion*, before slipping those same fingers underneath the T-shirt to appease his curiosity.

"Would you like some water yourself, Zion?"

Her question made him realize he'd been standing there assessing her thoroughly with his gaze. "No, thanks. I don't want any water."

He fought back the urge to say what was on his mind. *What I really want is you, Celine.* Deciding he needed to get the hell out of his kitchen before it became way too hot, he said, "I forgot to mention there's a courtesy bathrobe in your guest room closet."

"Oh, now you tell me."

He shoved his hands into the pockets of his jeans. "Yes, now I tell you." He backed up a few steps and said, "I'll see you in the morning," before he turned and left.

Celine released a deep sigh when Zion left the kitchen. She wondered if he knew that he wore sexual desire on his sleeve even when shirtless. She'd recognized the ragged heat in his gaze and noticed the huge erection pressing against his zipper, something he hadn't tried to hide. She figured he couldn't have hidden it even if he'd wanted to. She hadn't wanted her eyes to wander below his waist, but found herself doing so anyway, fascinated that he could desire her as much as she desired him.

She took another sip of water, needing it to cool down her body. She still couldn't understand how he could cause such rapid and intense fire to rush through her veins just from looking at her. He had stood less than five feet away, shirtless, with jeans riding low on his hips, in his bare feet, with a headful of dreadlocks flowing around his shoulders. *Sexy* couldn't come close to describing how he looked or how him staring at her had made her feel.

Celine knew she should go to bed and try to get some sleep. The majority of the night was gone and it would be morning soon. Then she would leave. Just where she would go, she wasn't sure, but it had to be someplace other than here. Temptation was too alive and appealing within these walls for her to even think about staying.

But then, he hadn't invited her to stay beyond tonight, so that meant he wanted her gone, too. For them to make love—no matter how enticing the thought—would be a huge mistake. She had enough to worry about than to indulge in a casual affair with Zion.

Why did he have to be one of the finest men she'd ever met? Just his walk alone could give her total heart failure. And his smile, when he cared to show it, was a jolt to any woman's hormones. Even his serious side was a total turn-on. If she could think of any part of his behavior as a turnoff she wouldn't be here. However, he'd been the first person who'd come to mind when she'd needed a safe place.

She did feel safe here, and not just because it was a secured residence. She felt safe because of Zion. She didn't want to think how tonight could have ended up differently had she not decided to take matters into her own hands and escape. She had no idea where she was being taken or how long she would have been held. Celine could and would admit she'd been petrified of the possible outcome, but had managed to keep her cool.

After washing out her glass, she placed it on the counter. She was feeling clean, refreshed and rather sleepy. Leaving the kitchen, she headed for the bedroom Zion was letting her use, to grab a few winks.

The ringing of the phone awakened Zion. It was his burner phone and not his regular cell. That meant the call wasn't from Alessandro. Pulling himself up in bed, Zion reached for it. The call was from the last number that had been dialed, which meant it was Levy Michaels.

Easing out of bed with the ringing phone in his hand, Zion quickly grabbed his other phone, as well, before walking down the hall to the room Celine was using, and knocked a few times before he heard her sleepy "Come in."

After opening the door, he stopped dead in his tracks. She was lying on top of the covers, on her side, with half her face buried in a pillow and his T-shirt barely covering her shapely thighs. Seeing her bare flesh made the lower part of his body throb with need.

"Celine?"

As if the sound of his voice cut through her sleep haze, she lifted her head, and when she saw him standing in the doorway, she let out a startled squeal before quickly getting beneath the bedcovers.

"I knocked and you told me to come in," he said, feeling it was something he should remind her of.

"I know. Sorry about that, but for a minute I'd forgotten where I was. I'm used to our housekeeper, Aggie, coming in to wake me every morning."

If Aggie found her in a similar position in her bed each morning, he would eagerly trade places with the woman. "Oh, I see." And he had seen enough to get his libido revved.

"Is there a reason you needed to see me, Zion?"

Her question made him remember the phone, which was now silent. "The burner phone was ringing. I believe it was your father calling you back."

"Oh," she said, quickly sitting up. "I'll call him now."

Zion crossed the room to hand it to her, and was about to turn to leave when she said, "No, please stay. Depending on what he says, I might need a voice of reason again. I'm still upset about this."

And the more he thought about it, the more he felt she should be upset. "Okay."

She scooted over for him to sit on the edge of the bed as she redialed the number and placed the phone on speaker.

"Celine?"

"Dad? I see you tried calling me."

"Yes, for a minute I was worried," Levy said.

"What is it, Dad?"

"I spoke with Nikon. It seems those guys that snatched you had come up with their own plans to ensure he paid them the money he owed."

"Which was?"

"To do like they told you—hold you until he did."

"And what if he didn't pay them?"

There was a pause, and when her father didn't answer, she repeated the question in a fiercer tone. "What if he didn't pay them, Dad?"

"If he didn't pay, then they were going to hit me up for ransom, in the amount he owed them. You did the right thing by getting away, but according to Nikon, they aren't happy with it."

"Too bad," Celine said, and Zion watched a smug, mocking smile touch her lips.

"I was told they are looking for you."

"Who are they? I didn't want to contact the authorities until I talked to you. I should contact them to try and stop them," she said.

"Right now it's not a good idea to get the police involved."

"Why not?"

A deep frown settled on Celine's face when her father didn't answer right away. "I asked why not?" she repeated.

"Just think about it, Celine. Getting the authorities involved would be an international nightmare, a scandal of the worst proportions. Right now both our names are linked to Nikon. You as his fiancée, although technically you aren't, and then me as the primary investor in his next film project. I want to do what I agreed to do in the beginning, which was to give Nikon a week to handle his mess. Just so you know, I've notified the FBI, so they know what's going on. I'm not ready to file an official report of kidnapping, since you're now safe. However, they suggest that you stay put and out of sight for the time being. The only reason I'm taking this approach is because Nikon has assured me he will pay the debt, and according to you, you're in a safe place for now. It's just a matter of you extending your time in Rome a few more days."

Zion could feel Celine's anger. "It's more than me extending my time here, Dad. I am in hiding. There is a big difference. I will give Nikon a week to clear up this mess, otherwise I am going to the embassy. And at that point I won't give a damn about Nikon's reputation or your monetary investment. Do I make myself clear, Dad?"

"Yes, but—"

"No buts. I mean what I said."

"Fine. I'll call you with updates whenever I can. Within a week, when this is over, I'm coming to get you myself. Goodbye, sweetheart."

"Bye, Dad." She clicked off the phone.

Celine looked over at Zion. "You heard."

"Yes, I heard."

"As soon as I can, I'll leave and—"

"And go where?" he asked her. "I heard your father,

and you heard him, too, Celine. Those men are looking for you."

"I know that, Zion, but what do you suggest? I can't stay here."

He was about to speak when his intercom buzzed. Using his cell phone, Zion clicked on. "Yes, Parker?"

"Mr. Rossi is here to see you, sir. Should I send him on up?"

"Yes, please do."

Clicking off the phone, he said to Celine, "Alessandro Rossi is a good friend of mine. You might want to put on your bathrobe, since you should come out and thank him."

She lifted a brow. "Thank him for what?"

Zion stood and smiled down at her. "You'll see."

Chapter 11

Celine heard male voices when she left the guest bedroom, after taking the time to brush her teeth, wash her face and finger-comb her hair. Tightening the belt of the ankle-length velour bathrobe around her waist, she stepped into the living room. The moment she did so, two pairs of eyes turned to look at her.

"Good morning," she said to the stranger, who was just as tall as Zion. He was very handsome, with black hair, dark eyes, olive skin and a megawatt smile.

The man crossed the room to her. "Good morning, *signorina*. I'm Alessandro Rossi," he said, extending his hand.

She took it and returned his smile. "Nice meeting you, and I'm Celine Michaels."

"Nice meeting you, as well." The man released her hand, but not before she noticed keen interest in his eyes. She also noticed when he'd touched her that she hadn't felt the electric currents that sizzled her insides whenever Zion did.

"Celine, Alessandro is a good friend of mine who owed me a favor," Zion was saying. "A favor I collected on last night by asking him to deliver this."

When he stepped aside she saw what had been hidden behind him. "My luggage!" she exclaimed, moving forward.

"Yes, your luggage. My sister verifies that all your belongings are in there. She's the one who packed up all your things," Alessandro said, with his mega-smile still in place.

"Your sister? But how did she get in my room?" she asked in surprise.

Alessandro chuckled. "I'll let Zion explain."

She then turned questioning eyes to Zion, who said, "Alessandro's family owns the Inspiron Hotel, and I asked that all your belongings in the room be brought here to me. However, there is something you should know."

Celine could tell by the tone of Zion's voice that it was something she didn't want to hear. "What?"

"Alessandro noticed two men parked outside when he and Isabella arrived at the hotel this morning. He checked the hotel's security cameras, and it appears the men arrived last night around two and have been parked there since then."

Celine nodded. "That's around the same time I showed up here."

"It's a good thing you didn't go back to the hotel after you got away. Someone was ready to grab you again."

Celine shuddered at the thought. She then turned to Alessandro. "Were those men still there when you left?"

"Yes," he told her. "That's the reason Isabella and I went out the back way and used one of the hotel's unmarked vehicles to come here. I just phoned hotel security to check the cameras again, and the men are still parked outside.

I think they hope you'll eventually return to get your belongings."

"Let them keep thinking that," Zion said, in a tone so deadly Celine couldn't help glancing at him. When he stared back at her, she could feel his anger. She could also feel his desire, and their gazes locked and held for a period of time.

When Alessandro cleared his throat, she broke eye contact with Zion to glance over at him. A huge smile was on the man's face when he turned to Zion and said, "I'll be going. For helping me out I promised Isabella that I would treat her to breakfast. She is in the car waiting for me."

"Thank you, Alessandro, and please thank your sister for me," Celine said.

He switched his gaze from Zion to her. "I will. Goodbye, Celine, and stay safe."

"Wow, Zion, you didn't say she was such a beauty," Alessandro said as the two men stepped out the door and stood in the corridor.

Zion looked pointedly at his friend. "Didn't know I was supposed to."

"Hey, don't get territorial. I take it she's off-limits."

"She's off-limits to you. I know how you operate."

"Oh, so now you're vying to be her protector and not her lover."

"I'm not vying to be her anything."

"Well, she's going to need a protector. I saw those men, Zion. Even in business suits they look like ruffians. I don't know the whole story of what's going on, but I suggest you do whatever you can to keep her out of their hands."

"I will." It surprised Zion how quickly he'd spoken, but he meant what he said. He would protect Celine. Why such a thing was important to him, he wasn't sure. Maybe it had to do with that quick flash of fear he'd seen in her eyes when Alessandro had told them about those men parked outside the hotel, waiting for her to return.

"Good. If you hadn't decided to do so, I would have," Alessandro replied. "Like I said, she's beautiful."

"And like I said," Zion reiterated, "she's off-limits to you."

He didn't like it when Alessandro threw his head back and laughed. Deciding not to be the target of his friend's humor any longer, he said, "Don't keep Isabella waiting, and thank her for her assistance. And again, I thank you, as well."

Alessandro smiled. "No thanks needed, my friend."

When Zion returned from seeing Alessandro out, he could hear the water going in the guest bathroom and figured with the return of her belongings Celine had decided to take another shower and get dressed. He decided to use that time to shower himself, and then over breakfast they would discuss what their next move should be.

Their next move? By rights, whatever she was dealing with was her business, not his. He rubbed a hand down his face, wishing he could think that way, but like he'd told Alessandro, he would protect her. There had never been a time when he needed to step into the role of any woman's protector, but he knew he would do it for Celine without blinking an eye.

Going into his bedroom, he used his phone to order breakfast for two to be delivered thirty minutes from now. After that he stripped off his clothes, showered, then dressed in a pair of jeans and a sweatshirt. Leaving his bedroom, he headed for the kitchen to set the table, but stopped when he saw Celine sitting in his living room. She was dressed, with her luggage next to her, and stood when she saw him.

Zion tried not to focus on her outfit—a pair of boots,

a long, flowing skirt and a wool jacket. She looked good, but then, he would admit there had never been anything she'd worn around him that she hadn't looked appealing in. And just like before, sexual energy was zinging between them, making it hard for him to think about anything but his desire for her.

"I didn't want to leave before thanking you again and telling you goodbye."

"Goodbye? You heard what Alessandro said, Celine. People are looking for you."

"I know that, Zion, but I can't impose on you any longer. The Inspiron isn't the only hotel in Rome. I'll check into another one and wait it out. I'll use a fake name if I have to. Those men can't keep watch on every hotel in this city."

"Do you know for certain that they can't?"

"No, but I can't wait it out here."

She was right; she couldn't. The best thing to do was to get her out of the city for a while. "I agree, but not for the reason you assume." When the doorbell sounded, he said, "I ordered breakfast. We can talk about it while we eat."

Celine glanced across the table at Zion. They were half-way through breakfast and he had yet to bring up anything. In fact, other than ask if she'd slept well last night, he hadn't said much at all. Of course, she'd replied that she had, when she really hadn't. She had endured a very eventful night and should have been knocked out as soon as her head touched the pillow. Instead, her body had fought sleep, knowing she and Zion were under the same roof once again. Just knowing he was sleeping in a bed a few feet away from her had made sleep nearly impossible.

She glanced at her watch. It was nine o'clock already and she had decisions to make. She had checked and her phone was still out of service. The first thing she intended to do after leaving here was to try to get a new phone, preferably a burner. She looked over at Zion. "You wanted to talk, right?"

He took a sip of his coffee and looked up at her. She wished he hadn't. Once again her stomach fluttered, just as it always did whenever his dark eyes leveled on her.

He placed his coffee cup down and leaned back in his chair. "I think your best bet is to stay with me."

He had to be kidding. "I honestly don't think that's a good idea."

"Would you like to tell me why?"

He had to know very well why, but if he needed her to spell it out for him she would. "It seems that nothing has changed between us. We still manage to turn each other on. And frankly, I have a lot more to worry about than ending up in your bed."

He smiled, and the way his lips curved was drawing her in. She didn't want to be drawn in. She was in enough trouble already.

"You would only end up in my bed if you want to be there, Celine."

Like she wouldn't want to be there. The man was a human magnet. All he had to do was look at her and she could feel herself being drawn to him. "Denying desire when it comes to you is not that easy, Zion."

"Why not?"

Did his ego need stroking or something? "Because it's not."

He didn't reply for a minute and then said, "Let's think about this for a moment. Both realistically *and* sexually. Realistically, unless you know someone else in Rome you can trust, then I suggest you remain with me."

She sighed deeply. Her college friend who used to live in Rome had since married and was now living in Venice. "I don't know anyone. But like I told you, I can check into another hotel."

"Is that a chance you really want to take, Celine?"

No, it isn't. "I can't get you involved in this."

"I'm already involved."

"I'm trying to get you uninvolved, Zion. I have no idea what shady business dealings Nikon is mixed up in."

"It has to be something pretty damn bad for those men to think it was okay to kidnap you until he pays up. And just the thought that he went along with it pisses me off. What an ass."

In Celine's book Nikon was worse than an ass. "We've discussed 'realistically.' Now let's cover 'sexually.'"

He took another sip of his coffee and then said, "All right. Sexually, I agree not to jump your bones if you don't jump mine first."

She frowned. "And you think I'd try?"

He shrugged. "Wouldn't you? I recall you once boldly declaring that we would make love one day, and that it was a waste of good sexual energy for us not to."

Yes, she had said that, and at the time she'd meant it. The sexual energy was still there, even with all this danger surrounding her. Whenever he looked at her she was aware of his male power and strength. And it was power and strength that could jolt enough sexual energy to rock her to her core. Even now remembering their last kiss sent frissons of desire dancing down every nerve ending.

"Yes, I said it, and nothing has changed. I think you see that for yourself."

He nodded. "I can not only see it, I can feel it."

Celine could, too, and it was so deep, she was aware of it in every pore of her body. She could honestly admit that every single thing about Zion Blackstone turned her on. His nearness, his scent, his looks, the memory of his taste…

"I suggest you come up with a plan to combat this thing between us," he added, "because I don't intend to let you walk out that door when it's not safe for you to do so."

She took a sip of her own coffee. "Don't tell me you intend to kidnap me, as well."

A crooked smile touched his lips. "That doesn't sound like a bad idea, to tie you up and keep you here."

Tie her up. Why did an image of her being tied to his bed suddenly flash in her mind, sending pulsating need rushing through her? She banished the image and focused on what he'd said about a plan.

"A plan, huh? I just might have an idea."

He hoped it was a good one, because crackles of sexual energy were passing between them as she spoke. "What's your idea?"

"I think we should go ahead and sleep together. Just get it out of the way and be through with it."

He tilted his head questioningly. "Get it out of the way and be through with it?"

"Yes. Then all this sexual energy between us will go away."

Zion stared at her. Did she honestly think they could sleep together and the attraction would just dissipate? That was not how intense desire between two people worked. At least for him it didn't. Not when there was this relentless pounding in his crotch just from looking at her and inhaling her scent.

Desire was clawing at him, hot, sharp and deep. He was trying like hell to fight it, but found it difficult to do. Sitting across from her while she'd been eating, watching the movement of her mouth and wishing it was on a certain part of his anatomy, had been pure hell.

"Well, what do you think of that idea?" she asked him.

Zion felt that she deserved his honesty. "We could have fun trying, but it will take more than one time to purge us from each other's system."

"Why would you think that?"

Instead of answering, he reached across the table and traced his finger down her arm. Whatever sensations she felt from the touch, he was feeling, as well. He could see how desire was lighting up the dark pupils of her eyes and the way her breathing had changed.

When he removed his hand from her, she lifted her chin. "Okay, you've proved your point."

"Good. Now we can concentrate on leaving here."

She blinked. "Leave?" At his nod, she asked, "And go where?"

"To my home in the country. I don't like the thought of remaining in town when people are actively looking for you, especially in this area."

"What about your work? I don't want to interfere with that."

"You won't. I have workshops in both places, so it doesn't matter." There was no need to tell her the pieces he was working on were hers. Nor did she need to know the reason he'd gotten started on them was because she'd been on his mind practically every single day since returning from Los Angeles.

She nodded. "If you're sure about leaving, I'm already packed."

He stood. "Then it won't take me but a second to gather my things. It's an hour drive from here. I'll be back in a few minutes."

He went into his bedroom, closed the door and pulled

an overnight bag from the closet. Because he kept dual residences during most of the year, he kept clothes in both places, so he didn't need much. After packing up the few things he wanted to take, he pulled his cell phone out of his pocket and punched in a number.

York answered in a raspy voice. "Do you know what time it is in New York, Z?"

"Yes, I know. I need a favor." And as an ex-cop and now a security specialist, York was the perfect guy to go to.

"You in jail somewhere and need bail money?"

Zion chuckled. "No."

"Then this better be a matter of life or death."

"That's a possibility."

York was quiet for a minute and then said, "Hold on—I don't want to wake Darcy. I've discovered pregnant women need all the sleep they can get. I'm going into the living room."

Moments later York came back on the phone. "Okay, what the hell have you gotten yourself into, Z?"

"It's not me, but Celine Michaels. She's in Rome and last night she was kidnapped. Luckily, she got away from her abductors and came here."

"Where's here?"

"My place," Zion clarified.

"She's at your place? I heard on the news yesterday that she's engaged to that Greek-American actor, Nikon Anastas."

"No, she's *not*," Zion said, a little sharper than he'd intended.

"Umm, interesting."

Zion knew how York's mind worked. "It's not what you think."

"Then tell me what it is, Z. And at four in the morning New York time, it better be good."

Zion then relayed to York the situation as he knew it. "That's the story Levy Michaels is telling his daughter, but I have a feeling there's more to it than what he's saying. I want to know what's really going on."

"So do I. I agree that what he said about getting the FBI involved doesn't make sense when he doesn't want to get the authorities involved there in Rome. Notifying the FBI is basically the same thing as notifying the Italian authorities. It will all be official. I'll get on it right away and will let you know what I find out."

"Thanks, Y."

Chapter 12

Celine glanced at her watch. Had they been traveling for only an hour? It seemed like longer, probably because she was aware of every second she was in Zion's presence. Once they'd left the city he said she should relax, and even suggested that she take a nap, and that he would awaken her when they reached their destination.

That had been a good idea due to the little sleep she'd gotten the night before. However, each time she closed her eyes, she breathed in Zion's scent and her hormones started sizzling, making sleep the last thing on her mind.

For a while she had pretended sleep and studied him through slitted eyes, hoping he wouldn't catch her staring. He hadn't, but had pretty much kept his eyes on the road. She figured from the way he periodically checked the rearview and side mirrors that he was making sure they weren't being followed.

Even sitting behind the steering wheel his powerful, masculine body was eye-catching and totally absorbing.

Then there were his broad shoulders and bulging biceps. Why did he have to look so darn sexy and why did she feel obligated to notice?

Tired of feigning sleep, she sat up and stretched her neck to look out the window. It was only a matter of time before she was caught ogling him.

She couldn't help but admire the countryside they passed. Even with the season heading into winter, it was beautiful with lush green fields everywhere she looked. She bet come spring, flowers would be blooming all over the place.

Rome was behind them, and according to Zion, they were headed toward the charming town of Guadagnolo, where his country home was located on the outskirts. She figured hiding out a week should do it. For Zion to offer her protection was extremely kind and she didn't want to impose on him any longer than that.

"It's not too much farther. We will get there in time for lunch."

She glanced over at him. "Will we need to go to the market?"

"No. Since I'd planned to come here later this week, I contacted my caretaker a few days ago and asked him to stock up the place. However, he did so with my preferences in foods. There might be items you prefer eating that I won't have."

"I'm not hard to please."

"I recall you telling me that once before," he said in a throaty voice.

She remembered that time. That recollection made her glance over at him, and as if he'd anticipated her doing so, their gazes connected. Her breath caught at the heat she saw in his gaze, making a surge of yearning coil within her. "I hope you don't turn everything I say into a sexual innuendo, Zion."

"I'll try not to, Celine."

"And do you have to look at me like that?"

He shrugged his massive shoulders. "It's no different than the way I noticed you looking at me."

True, but did he have to point it out? "I don't know how we're going to last together for a week."

"I think you do."

She broke eye contact with him to glance back out the window. He was right. She did know. In fact, she was the one who'd suggested they just get it on and get it over with. However, he was the one who claimed his desires didn't operate on that premise.

That made her turn back to him and ask, "Why isn't there a serious woman in your life, Zion?"

"Why isn't there a serious man in yours, Celine?"

She should have expected his counterquestion, but hadn't. Regardless, it didn't matter, since the answer was simple. "I don't have the time."

He didn't say anything for a minute, just kept his eyes on the road, but she could tell he was rolling her response around in his head. "I guess all that shopping and jet-setting keeps you pretty busy."

She tried not to let it bother her that, like a lot of people, he thought that was all she did. He would be surprised to know about Second Chances. She could set him straight now, but she wouldn't. Let him think whatever he pleased. "I guess you can say that," she said. "Does that mean the reason you're not involved seriously with anyone is because a relationship would take too much time away from your jewelry designs?"

"No, they are mutually exclusive. I date when I want to. It's not a top priority for me. Some women expect to have bonded with you after a certain number of dates. Some even expect daily phone contact. Then there are others who honestly anticipate you asking them to move in after a while. None of that will happen with me."

"That's not all women's expectations. Some are happy with casual relationships."

When he brought the car to a stop at a crossroad, he glanced over at her. "Is that what you and Nikon Anastas have? A casual relationship?"

She rolled her eyes. "Nikon and I didn't have a relationship at all. It was all pretense to give the tabloids something to gossip about. We've covered this before, Zion."

"And you were satisfied with that? Having the tabloids print untrue stuff about you and him?"

"Yes, because we both knew none of it was accurate. But for Nikon to announce we were engaged definitely crossed the line."

"I would say it did more than cross the line. Appears it made you bait for his creditors." Zion shook his head. "You sure know how to pick them."

She narrowed her gaze and regretted that she couldn't see his eyes. "I did not pick Nikon. My father did. Like I said, it was a PR move."

"And you meekly went along with it?"

Although she hadn't liked what he'd said, she couldn't deny it was the truth. "I live in Hollywood, where relationships between couples are fabricated all the time. Publicity is the name of the game. The more of it you get the more your career can be advanced. Dad wanted to show a friendly connection between him and Nikon, and for us to appear to be dating was one way to do it. I wasn't seeing anyone at the time and didn't have a problem going along with the PR move they'd proposed."

"Well, it seems more like a PR move that's gone bad."

She had to agree with him on that. "I'm sure things will be fine once Nikon pays those people the money he owes them."

"Still, they had no right to kidnap you. And what if he doesn't pay them? Then what?"

Celine didn't want to think of that possibility. "Then they need to deal with him directly and keep me out of it."

"He should not have involved you in the first place. He literally tossed you to the wolves."

She didn't want to agree, but she had to. Nikon had pretty much shown he didn't give a crap about her well-being. She was tired of talking about her predicament and decided it was time to turn the conversation back to him. "When was the last time you had a steady girl?"

"Steady girl or steady bed partner?"

"Either. When was the last time?"

"Years ago. Steady or unsteady, they all knew Zion's Rules."

"Which are?"

"There are several. I told you about the not-mixing-business-with-pleasure rule while I was in Los Angeles. Then there's my rule that any woman entering into a relationship with me must know she can't change how I feel and what I think. I let them know up front that I don't believe in happily-ever-after, marriage or long-term relationships. I believe in living my life as a bachelor to the fullest, and I intend to do so for the rest of my days."

"Why don't you believe in happily-ever-after, marriage or long-term relationships?"

"Do I need a reason?"

"I think so. Having a stable of willing women at your beck and call will eventually get old, don't you think?"

"For some people, but not for me. I have no problem having a revolving door to my bedroom, and I make no excuses or apologies for doing so. Women are told up front that I am not a forever kind of guy. If they conveniently forget, that's their problem, not mine."

Celine studied his features. Was he putting her on alert? Letting her know that if they ever made it to his bed or hers, a roll between the sheets was all she'd ever get from him? "You said your five godbrothers are married, right?"

"Yes."

"You're happy for them?"

"Of course. Why wouldn't I be? They met and fell in love with nice women."

"However, you don't think it can happen to you? That you could meet and fall in love with a nice woman?"

"No."

His answer sounded pretty final and quick. He hadn't even paused to think about what she'd asked him. She wondered what had happened in his life to make him feel that way. Did his parents have a bad marriage?

She recalled he'd said his mother had died close to nine years ago. She also remembered that he'd moved to Rome shortly after her passing. Did he and his father not have a good relationship? Had his parents endured an unhappy marriage? It really wasn't any of her business, but there had to be a reason he was so antimarriage.

Although she was not interested in marriage or a serious involvement now, Celine had no problem with settling down and getting married one day. And it would be to a man of her own choosing. She would not let her father dictate what he thought was the perfect man for her like her maternal grandparents had done to her mother.

"Tell me about your parents, Zion."

She could tell from the immediate tightening of his jaw that she'd hit a sore spot. He slowed down the speed of the car and glanced at her with narrowed eyes. "Why do you want to know anything about my mom and dad?"

"Just trying to figure you out. There has to be a reason you're so against marriage."

Not for the first time, Zion thought Celine was too astute for her own good. "Why can't it be that I just don't want marriage and it has nothing to do with my parents?"

She shrugged. "Because usually if people come from a

happy home where both parents love each other, it's easier to accept that sort of relationship for themselves."

He wondered if perhaps that was true, because he definitely had trust issues when it came to women. He knew those issues had developed after he'd found out his mother had betrayed his father. Of all his godparents, he would say Virgil's parents were the couple who most enjoyed displaying open affection, even after over thirty years of marriage. Virgil's father still referred to his wife as his queen.

"I don't see you making any wedding plans, Celine. Didn't *your* parents have a good marriage?" he asked, in an attempt to shift the conversation from him to her.

"It depends on what you mean by *good*," she said, glancing at him when he brought his SUV to a stop at a traffic light.

He'd found her response interesting. "Weren't they happy together?"

She shrugged. "I guess you can say they tried to make the best of it. My maternal grandparents met my father and decided he would be a fine husband for their daughter, regardless of the fact that she was in love with someone else. A guy she'd met at college. They gave her an order as to who to marry and she obeyed."

"A marriage of convenience?"

"Yes." Celine took a breath, then explained. "I think Dad eventually fell in love with Mom, but I'm not sure she ever fell in love with him. I truly believed that until the day she died her heart belonged to another man."

As the traffic light changed, he asked, "And knowing your mother didn't love your father doesn't bother you?"

"No."

He didn't miss the firmness in her tone. "Why not?"

"I'm told Dad knew my mother was in love with another man, yet he married her anyway. I guess he assumed she would eventually fall in love with him."

She said it like it hadn't mattered one way or the other to

her that her parents hadn't loved each other. Zion guessed not being in love was different from not being faithful. His father loved his mother and had assumed the feelings were mutual. They hadn't been. Otherwise, she would not have done what she did. He couldn't help wondering what was worse: a loveless marriage or an adulterous one.

He turned off the major highway onto a two-lane narrow roadway that led to his villa. The road reached a steep incline, and when he hit level ground again he brought the vehicle to a stop. "Look to your right."

She did, and he saw the moment her eyes grew bright and her lips parted in awe. He smiled. He liked observing a person's first reaction when seeing his countryside home.

"Is that your place?" she asked, staring at him before returning her gaze to the window.

"Yes, that's mine. All ten acres, including the waterway it sits on. This is where I come when I need peace and quiet."

"And I'm invading your space."

"As you can see, it's plenty big for the both of us." He meant that. She could have her own wing and not be underfoot.

"I can't imagine you not getting lonely here by yourself."

"Imagine it, because I don't." He studied her mouth and wished he wasn't so focused on her lips. "You can have your very own suite. There are several. You can take your pick." And he hoped it was the one farthest from the master suite. "And, Celine?"

"Yes?"

"You are safe here."

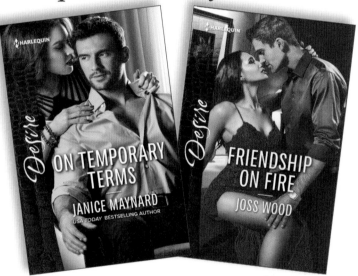

Dear Reader,

Since you are a lover of our books, your opinions are important to us... and so is your time.

That's why we made sure your **"FAST FIVE" READER SURVEY** can be completed in just a few minutes. Your answers to the five questions will help us remain at the forefront of women's fiction.

And, as a thank-you for participating, we'd like to send you **4 FREE THANK-YOU GIFTS!**

Enjoy your gifts with our appreciation,

Pam Powers

To get your
4 FREE THANK-YOU GIFTS:

✱ Quickly complete the "Fast Five" Reader Survey
and return the insert.

"FAST FIVE" READER SURVEY

1 Do you sometimes read a book a second or third time? ○ Yes ○ No

2 Do you often choose reading over other forms of entertainment such as television? ○ Yes ○ No

3 When you were a child, did someone regularly read aloud to you? ○ Yes ○ No

4 Do you sometimes take a book with you when you travel outside the home? ○ Yes ○ No

5 In addition to books, do you regularly read newspapers and magazines? ○ Yes ○ No

YES! I have completed the above Reader Survey. Please send me my 4 FREE GIFTS (gifts worth over $20 retail). I understand that I am under no obligation to buy anything, as explained on the back of this card.

225/326 HDL GM3T

FIRST NAME   LAST NAME

ADDRESS

APT.#   CITY

STATE/PROV.   ZIP/POSTAL CODE

Chapter 13

You are safe here...

Celine thought about what Zion had said as he pulled his vehicle into the circular driveway, brought the SUV to a stop and got out. Was she really safe here? Possibly from those men trying to find her, but what about from him? Even if he banished her to another wing in this monstrosity of a house, they would still be under the same roof.

She unsnapped her seat belt when he opened the car door for her. Reaching out, he took hold of her hand to help her from the vehicle, and the instant he did so, her stomach muscles tightened and a jolt of electricity zapped her.

She'd glanced up into his eyes and knew from the way he was staring back at her that he had experienced the sensations, as well. The mutual feelings were so overwhelming, they stood there staring at each other for a long moment before he said, "Welcome to my country home, Celine."

She smiled. "Thank you, Zion."

"Let's get you inside." With his palm at the center of

her back, he guided her toward the huge front door. The feel of his hand on her seemed to burn her skin, until he removed it to open the door. She released the breath she'd been holding. Then he moved aside for her to step over the threshold. She'd always thought her father's home was beautiful, but this had a jaw-dropping appeal.

"I'll bring in your luggage."

He left her alone and she continued to glance around, admiring the structure, architecture and decor. The beauty of it all nearly overwhelmed her, and she shook her head at the thought that all this was just for one man. A man who had no intention of ever marrying or having a family. A man who was a renowned jeweler by trade and a loner by choice.

"I'll take these up to the guest room I think would be perfect for you to use," he said, returning with her bags. She had a hunch it would be as far away from his bedroom as possible.

"Thanks," she said, then added, "and you have a beautiful home, Zion."

"Thank you. I'll show you around when I get back."

She watched him head for the staircase with her luggage and then thought of something. "Zion?"

He turned and lifted a brow. "Yes?"

"Did you bring your burner phone? There are a couple of people I need to call."

"A couple of people?"

She saw the inquisitiveness in his eyes and said, "Yes. One is my best friend, Desha. I was supposed to return home today and she will wonder why I didn't. I don't want her to worry. And the other person is another friend of mine."

There was no need to tell him about Stuart Mosely, the person in charge of operations at Second Chances. There was an executive meeting scheduled for this week.

Instead of canceling it, she wanted the meeting to go on without her.

Zion pulled the phone out of his back pocket and passed it to her. The moment their hands touched it was as if a torch was lit and fire ignited into flames. The next thing she knew, Zion pulled her into his arms, crushing her against him and devouring her mouth.

Without missing a beat, her body responded. Immediately, she kissed him just as greedily as he did her. She could honestly admit she wanted this kiss. She needed it. It was something she had dreamed of over the past month, and now that she had the chance, she had no intention of letting this opportunity pass by without seizing the moment.

She had shared kisses with men before, but none provided the excitement and pleasure that kissing Zion always gave her. She was convinced she was becoming addicted to his taste. That was the only way she could explain why she was as much into this kiss as he was. Why she was allowing his hands to roam all over her while he held her mouth captive, and why the feel of his hard erection pressing against her was really getting to her where it counted.

As if of their own volition, her hips began gyrating against him, and it felt as if his erection suddenly got harder and fuller, even more massive.

Suddenly, the sound of a grandfather clock marking the noon hour with a succession of loud chimes echoed throughout the room. Zion slowly ended the kiss, taking his time before separating their mouths. Then he gave her lips a lingering lick before saying, "We arrived in time for lunch."

"Yes, we did." She licked her own lips, not caring it was sending out the message that she'd enjoyed their kiss. She didn't care, because she *had* enjoyed it.

He was staring hard at her mouth, and knowing he was doing so made the pulse at the base of her throat throb.

"If you let me know where I'll be sleeping tonight, I can get settled. I would love for you to show me around later."

It was then that he dropped his hands from around her waist and took a step back. Immediately, she missed the warmth and hardness of the body that had been pressing close to hers. "And I want to show you around. Come on. Let's go up the stairs," he said, grabbing hold of her luggage again.

He led the way and she followed. They passed a bedroom with huge double doors, and Celine figured it was his. Instead of banishing her to another wing like she'd figured he would, he was planting her right across the hall from him.

They entered the bedroom and she glanced around, appreciating its beauty. There was a large window that overlooked a tennis court below and a huge lake out back. She looked over at Zion and it was easy to see his erection hadn't gone down yet. Focusing on his face and not the lower part of his body, she said, "This is a beautiful room, Zion."

He nodded. "Thanks. I figured you would appreciate this one over any of the others because of the view. However, if you see another guest room you prefer while we're touring, just let me know."

Celine doubted that would be happening. The main reason she liked this room was because his bedroom was right across the hall. She switched her gaze from the view out the window to where Zion was standing with his hands shoved into the pockets of his jeans. "I love this room and see no reason I won't be satisfied sleeping here."

He nodded. "I'll leave you to get settled and to make those calls. When you finish you can join me downstairs. I'll take you on a tour before we do lunch."

"All right."

When he closed the door behind him, she released a deep sigh. She'd been in Zion's home less than ten minutes and already they'd shared a kiss that still had her heart pounding. She had a feeling that had just been the beginning.

As Zion walked down the stairs, he wondered why he was letting Celine Michaels get to him. First of all, she was invading his space, although he'd denied to her that she was doing so. A woman or two might have gotten invited to his condo, but he didn't bring any women here.

More than one had called him an ass for the way he would turn off passion once he was certain they'd both been satisfied. Zion had no desire to cuddle after sex. After the lovemaking ended he felt it was time for his bed partner to leave if they were at his place, or for him to haul ass if he was at hers. As a rule, he didn't spend the entire night with a woman, and didn't invite one to spend an entire night with him. That was the way he operated, and he had no intention of changing.

His godbrothers figured he was that way because of the one time he'd dozed off after having sex, only to wake up and find the woman searching his room as if she thought he'd have a piece of jewelry lying around with her name on it. That wasn't it, and he'd told them that more than once. Yet they remained optimistic that his attitude regarding women would eventually change. He knew for certain it wouldn't.

The moment he entered his kitchen he started the coffee maker, loving the smell of fresh coffee brewing.

A short while later he was just about to take a sip when Celine entered. The cup froze halfway to his lips when he glanced up and saw her waltzing into his kitchen like she belonged there. He wasn't exactly sure how he felt about that.

"Would you like some coffee?" he asked, pushing the troubling thought to the back of his mind.

"Yes, please."

He didn't have to ask her how she liked her coffee, since he remembered from that morning at breakfast. But pouring the coffee did little to take his mind off how she looked standing in the middle of his kitchen. He'd liked the outfit she was wearing this morning and liked it more on her now. The long, flowing skirt swished around her booted legs when she walked. And he wasn't imagining it; there was definitely an erotic sway to her hips as she came to stand in front of him. He quickly fought for control of his rapid breathing and heartbeat.

"I'm returning your burner phone," she said, placing it on the counter instead of putting it in his hand. They both knew why she'd decided to do that.

"I trust you made your calls."

"Yes. Thanks for letting me use it."

"You're welcome."

Instead of following her lead and placing the coffee cup on the counter beside the burner phone, he handed it to her. "Here you are."

He watched her draw in a deep breath before reaching for the mug. "Stop being hard on yourself, Celine," he said. "It is what it is and neither of us can do anything about it."

Their fingers brushed and the desire that flashed in her eyes made his heart race. No man should want a woman as much as he wanted her, and knowing the yearning was mutual didn't help matters.

He took a sip of his coffee and, over the rim of his cup, watched her take a drink of hers. He hadn't known until that morning at breakfast that observing a woman drinking coffee could be arousing. But it was more than just the way her lips were fitting on her cup. It was also her scent and the way she was looking at him.

"Mmm, this is good," she said, licking her lips. She'd done the same thing after their kiss, which meant she'd thought their kiss had been good, as well.

"Glad you like it." He checked his watch and then looked back at her. "Ready for that tour?"

She nodded. "Yes, I'm ready."

He started downstairs, showing her the guest room on the main floor, as well as the dining room and living room that she'd seen earlier. What she hadn't seen was the indoor pool and spa, as well as the glassed-in, climate-controlled patio.

On the second floor, in addition to Zion's bedroom, which he merely pointed out but didn't take her into, were two other guest rooms, each with their own exquisite bath, and a movie theater. The third floor jutted out into wings, with two additional guest bedroom suites in each. There was also a game room up there, with a huge pool table in the center.

"You entertain a lot, I take it?"

"No. As I mentioned earlier, I like solitude. However, my godbrothers and godparents come visit on occasion." There was no need to tell her that when he'd first moved to Rome they'd done so rather frequently. He'd always been glad to see everyone, but knew the visits had mainly been to check on him. His godparents couldn't understand why he'd moved so far from home, and his godbrothers were concerned about his state of mind.

"Now to give you a tour of the outside. You might want to grab a jacket, given that the temperature has dropped since we got here. I'll wait for you downstairs."

"All right."

He was standing at the bottom of the steps when she came down a little later, carrying a short, black leather jacket. He released a drawn-out sigh. How long would it take for him not to get turned on just looking at her?

He was tempted to take her hand as he led her toward the door, but refrained from doing so. There was no need to throw grease onto an already-blazing flame. Instead, they walked side by side through his flower garden.

"The flowers are beautiful. How do you get them to bloom during the winter months?"

He glanced at his flower beds filled with camellias, azaleas and roses. "That's one of the things I found fascinating about living in this region of Italy. Flowers tend to bloom all twelve months of the year. It has something to do with the humid continental climate that's found up here in the hills and mountains. I think of it as one of nature's wonders."

They continued walking through the flower gardens to an area in the back where a huge waterfall was located. "This was one of the reasons I bought this house. I was sold the moment I saw this," he said, coming to a stop in front of the fall.

"I can see why. It's beautiful. I can envision coming out here every morning and sitting over there to drink my coffee. I would find it so relaxing."

He did, too. Not only did he often drink his coffee out here, but on occasion he ate meals here, as well. There was something about the sound of rushing water that soothed any turbulence flowing through him. Too bad it wasn't doing anything about the sexual desire consuming him. He just didn't understand it. He'd never been this taken with a woman. Never been this physically attracted to one.

Deciding it was best if they kept moving, he led her down several steps into a courtyard. He stopped and pointed to a smaller two-story house. "That's where I make my jewelry. I converted that cottage into a workplace."

"It's massive."

"I need the space for my shop and lab. There's a small

kitchen, and also a bedroom and full bath on the second floor to use if I'm working late and just want to crash there."

"You work alone?"

"Yes, and I prefer it that way."

"Isn't that time-consuming?"

"Yes, but I don't overextend myself. At least not now. I admit in the beginning, when orders began rolling in, I was so excited that I continuously burned the midnight oil trying to fill them. But I refused to focus on quantity instead of quality and had to cut back. Now I'm working at a pace I'm satisfied with."

He checked his watch. "Are you ready for lunch?"

She met his gaze and nodded. "Yes, I'm ready, but only if you let me do the honors. I might not be the cook you are, but there are a few specialty dishes I can prepare. And since it's past lunchtime, we can consider this an early dinner."

Other than his godmothers when they'd come to visit, no women had ever taken control of his kitchen. He wasn't sure how he felt about one doing so now. Since she'd made the offer, though, he couldn't really turn her down without a legitimate reason, so he decided to go with the flow. "My kitchen is all yours."

Zion realized he'd just spoken words to her that he'd never intended to say to any woman.

Chapter 14

Celine thought Zion had a spacious kitchen and she moved about as if she'd done so several times. Her father would be shocked to discover she knew her way around anyone's kitchen, since she'd never shown any interest at home. What he didn't know was that she worked with various notable chefs who volunteered their time and services to Second Chances.

The burner phone, which was still sitting on the counter, rang. Celine had learned her lesson about being quick to answer it. When she'd done so a half hour or so ago, assuming it was her father, it had been someone for Zion. A woman name Bettina. Needless to say, it was quite obvious she hadn't appreciated another female answering Zion's phone. Since Bettina had called on the burner and not his regular cell phone, Celine didn't have to wonder just what type of relationship the two of them shared. That was why it hadn't bothered her one iota when the woman took time to try to convince Celine of how important Bettina was in Zion's life.

And speaking of Zion…

He had left a few hours ago for his workspace and hadn't returned. She'd given him an approximate time when dinner would be ready, and it was past that time and he still hadn't shown up.

His phone stopped ringing and she checked it to verify that it had been Bettina and not her father. When she saw it had been the woman, she placed the phone back on the counter.

Her thoughts shifted to her dad. She hadn't talked to him again since that morning. Knowing he had notified the FBI had given her some assurance he was taking things seriously. When she'd spoken with Desha earlier, she hadn't told her best friend about the kidnapping. She merely told her that she'd decided to extend her stay in Rome another week.

Celine was glad she'd checked in at Second Chances, as well. Stuart had assured her things were running smoothly as usual. When she'd told him that she'd decided to extend her trip to Europe for another week, he had encouraged her to enjoy herself. If only he knew how impossible that would be to do.

"Something smells good."

Celine turned from the stove to glance over at Zion. Desire rushed through her insides the instant she saw him. She would think the sexual chemistry between them would have lessened by now, but it hadn't. If anything, it was stronger than ever. "I hope it tastes as good as it smells."

"I'm sure it will. What is it?"

"A chicken potpie. I found all the ingredients I needed here. Your caretaker did an awesome job of stocking the place."

"He usually does," Zion said, walking over to the sink to wash his hands. "What can I do to help?"

Celine should be happy he offered his assistance, but sharing space with him wouldn't work. Regardless of how massive his kitchen was, he seemed to draw her to him. "No help needed. I got this. Besides, you got a call on your burner phone you might want to return. I made the mistake of answering it, thinking my dad was calling. Instead it was your friend Bettina. I don't think she appreciated hearing my voice."

She watched Zion intently to see if what she'd said had any effect on him. Instead, as he grabbed a towel off the counter to dry his hands, his expression remained unchanged. To be certain he'd heard her, she added, "She called twice, in fact. I didn't answer the second time. I let it go as a missed call."

"That's fine," he finally said.

If he thought that was the end of it, then he was sorely mistaken. Why she suddenly felt a twinge of jealousy now and hadn't before when she'd talked to Bettina earlier, she wasn't sure. It might be because now that she was looking at Zion, she was thinking of him and this Bettina together sharing a bed, of Bettina touching him in places that Celine only dreamed of touching, of him sinking into Bettina's body instead of hers, and sharing a piece of himself with Bettina that he hadn't shared with Celine.

Or she could accept the jealousy she felt was the result of seeing him and being reminded of what a good-looking, fine-ass man he was. A man with a perfect body and great set of bones. Bones she had no problem jumping. Regardless of the reason for her envious state, she needed to hear him say again that he wasn't seriously interested in any woman. Even if that included her. She needed to hear him repeat Zion's Rules, proclaiming he was a bachelor for life.

She took the potpie out of the oven and placed it on the stove top to cool. Out the corner of her eye she saw Zion cross the kitchen to the refrigerator and open it. For some reason she couldn't let the call from the other woman go, and said, "Bettina had a lot to say."

"Did she?"

She glanced over at him and wished she hadn't. He was leaning against the counter with a water bottle to his lips. When did the act of a man drinking water become sexy as hell? "Yes."

After taking a huge gulp, he lowered the bottle, met her gaze and asked, "What about?"

Celine swallowed deeply, trying to focus on his eyes and not on his wet lips. Why was she tempted to cross the room and lick them dry? "She pretty much warned me to keep my hands off you."

He held her gaze for the longest time. She licked her lips, and when he mimicked her action, she felt a tightening in her stomach. If that wasn't bad enough, the intense desire she saw in his eyes had her heart racing and made the juncture of her thighs throb relentlessly.

He took another swig of water before placing the empty bottle on the counter. Not breaking eye contact with her, he asked, "Do you intend to heed her warning, Celine?"

She swallowed again and then decided that with this conversation honesty was the best policy. "I don't want to."

"Then don't. And just for the record, you can put your hands on me whenever, however and wherever you like."

Zion meant it.

A sensual tightness settled in his chest as he stared at Celine. He liked the way her hair flowed in a silky wave around her shoulders, framing a long, graceful neck. And why did he have a thing when it came to her lips? Maybe it was the way they were shaped, as if they'd been made just for kissing.

He couldn't help but notice she was checking him out like he was doing with her. He hoped that, like him, she was finally done with fighting this thing between them. Ready to throw in the towel and replace it with silken sheets. Earlier, he had deliberately gone to his work cottage. Once there he'd discovered that he couldn't concentrate one bit. His head had been filled with thoughts of her. He couldn't get out of his mind all the things he wanted to do to her, but was fighting hard not to. And it hadn't helped matters that it had been her jewelry he'd been working on.

He had given up trying to stay focused, and had returned to the main house. Intense heat had consumed him the moment he'd walked into his kitchen and seen her. Why did she look so good in here? So much at home? Maybe it had something to do with the fact that she was in bare feet and wearing one of his aprons.

She took a step toward him, then stopped. He knew she was trying to decide what to do, certain she remembered his rules. That meant whatever they started would be finished when she left here. There would be no follow-up calls, no texting and no attempts at a long-distance romance. In other words, once she returned to LA, there would be no staying in touch.

Sensing her indecisiveness, he asked, "Need help?"

She held his gaze. "With what?"

"With any decisions you're trying to make."

She angled her head. "And you think you can help me make them?"

"I can certainly try."

He watched her lick her lips again before she asked, "How?"

Zion was hoping she would ask. He moved toward her,

keeping his gaze focused on her eyes. When he came to a stop in front of her he wrapped his arms around her waist and pulled her body closer to his. He was certain she'd seen his erection the entire time, but now she felt it pressed hard against her. He wanted her to feel it because he wanted her to know just what she was doing to him.

"This is how." He lowered his head to hers, and the moment his mouth touched her lips, fire blazed through his loins.

He loved her taste and latched on to her mouth to savor it. From the way their tongues were tangling, it was as if their earlier kiss had only whetted their appetite for each other. They weren't kissing; their mouths were mating. That was the only way he could describe the slow, deliberate, intense and bold assault of her mouth by his.

This kiss was quickly becoming scandalous. He was tempted to stake a claim to her entire body, here and now. But he wanted to let his tongue play with hers, suck on it, torment it and devour it a little while longer. Her moan was sensual music to his ears, and when she began pressing the lower part of her body against his hard erection, he knew what would eventually happen if she kept it up.

Hell, he wanted it to happen. He was too far gone to stop and hoped she was, too. From the way she was kissing him back he knew that she was almost there. He reluctantly broke off the kiss and proceeded to lick around her mouth, which made her moan even more. He loved the sound. It was sexy and made him simmer inside.

Zion pulled back and gazed down at her. This was the woman he wanted. Not Bettina, Katrina, Deborah or the last woman he'd had sex with, someone name Danelle. None of them mattered. Only her. And a bolt of fire lanced through him at the thought of having her. Sinking into her moist depths, raking his fingers across the nipples of her breasts and absorbing all her heat.

"You know what I want?" he asked her in a low voice.

She reached up and traced his lips with her fingertips. "I have an idea."

He had a feeling her idea would be right on the mark. "Assuming your idea is correct, what do you say to that?"

She wrapped her arms around his neck. "I say bring it on, Zion Blackstone, if you are so bold."

He was so bold. Suddenly, he swept her off her feet and into his arms. Leaving the kitchen, he headed toward the stairs.

Chapter 15

Celine was in such a sensuous daze she hadn't realized Zion had brought her into the guest room instead of taking her across the hall to his bedroom. When he placed her in the middle of the bed and then leaned down and recaptured her lips, she became so caught up in the warm, silky taste of his mouth that it didn't really matter whose room they used, as long as it had a bed.

If she had had her way, they would never have made it up the stairs. They could have used the sofa, the rug in front of the fireplace or the steps. The place would not have mattered to her, just as long as he was inside her. She needed him and she needed him now.

She had thought about this moment. Had dreamed about it. Had awakened in the middle of some nights, yearning for it and regretting what had not happened when he'd been in Los Angeles.

Not again and not this time. He would discover she

was a woman who went after what she wanted—and she wanted him. She knew the score and accepted his rules. Now he would have to accept that some rules were meant to be broken. He had broken one before, and if needed, she figured he could certainly break a few more.

He pulled back from the kiss and stared at her. In her mind, she could hear the minutes ticking by as he did so. But she wouldn't rush him. He could take his time, because in the end she would get what she wanted and he would get what he wanted, as well. There was no happily-ever-after for them, and she understood and accepted that. But whether they liked it or not, there was this thing between them that neither could control, tame or deny. All they had was now, and she intended to make this moment everything they desired and more.

"I want you, Celine," he said, in a deep, throaty voice. "But I need to make sure there won't be any misunderstandings between us. I need to be certain you fully understand my rules."

Zion's Rules. She held his gaze and figured this was the spiel he gave to every woman before sharing his body with her. He needed to make sure they not only understood but accepted.

"You told me what they were and I understand and accept them, because I have no desire to continue anything with you beyond our time together here."

She figured that should have made him happy, and couldn't understand the frown that darkened his features. Did he think he was the only one who could institute rules? "Why, Celine?"

He had the nerve to ask her why? After shoving his rules down women's throats? "My main reason is my love of myself. I prefer not to deal with men who are heartbreakers. Been there. Done that. And I have no intentions of traveling that road again."

He continued to stare at her, but said nothing. Neither did she. There was nothing either of them could say, since they fully understood each other. When time passed and they continued to sit there and stare, she finally did something she'd never done before. She reached out and copped a feel of him through his jeans. "I hope this is not going to go down while you're trying to figure me out, Zion."

He reached down and placed his hand on hers. "No. In fact, now that you touched me there, I'm convinced it's gotten bigger."

She noticed he was right about that and could actually feel it extending beneath her hand through the material of his jeans. "I think we have too many clothes on, don't you?"

"Yes, I think so, too."

She watched him slide off the bed. If he was going to do a strip show she intended to pay close attention to every single detail. Evidently he had other ideas how he intended to do things, and reached out and took her hand, drawing her to her feet. She tried ignoring the heated sensations that rushed through her from his touch.

"You undress me and I'll undress you," he suggested, smiling down at her.

"That will work," she said. Without wasting any time, she took hold of his T-shirt, pulled it over his head and tossed it aside. Then she did the very thing she'd wanted to do when she had seen him last night shirtless, standing in the doorway of his condo. She buried her face in his chest and breathed in his scent. He smelled so darn good.

She finally lifted her head to meet his inquisitive gaze. "Your scent turns me on."

That got a smile from him. "Your scent turns me on,

as well," he said, reaching out and pulling her blouse over her head. "But I'm more of a touchy sort of guy," he said, quickly freeing her breasts by dispensing with her bra. "I could never understand why women bother with bras."

Honestly? She could give him a ton of reasons, but not today. And when he lowered his head to her chest, she thought he was about to take a whiff of her scent like she'd done to him. Instead he sucked a nipple into his mouth, and she immediately felt weak in the knees. The warm pressure of his mouth was driving her insane, making her moan. And when he moved to the other nipple, she fought back a scream at the mindless, drugging kisses he was giving her breasts.

"Zion," she moaned, grabbing his head to tug on his locks to hold his mouth right there. And he delivered, cupping her breasts and kissing them with an openmouthed, wet urgency that rocked her to the core. What was he trying to do to her?

He finally released her breasts and lifted his head to stare up at her. The sound of her satisfied sigh whispered through the room. Had he not stopped when he had, there was no doubt in her mind she would have had a full-blown orgasm just from what he'd done to her breasts.

"Now to move on," he said, reaching out and releasing the clasp to her skirt. It slid to the floor, leaving her clad in a thong. The heat of his gaze roamed over her like a slow burn, causing a luscious ache to consume her. He then took hold of the waistband of her undies and bent to slide them down her legs.

"My turn," she said softly, reaching out to unzip his jeans. "I'm going to need your help with this," she said, seeing how the size of his erection would make things a little tricky.

"No problem," he said, taking over and tugging both jeans and boxer shorts down a pair of muscular thighs.

Her mouth literally dropped open upon seeing the size of him. She'd known from the feel of him that he was big, but he wasn't just big—he was colossal. And that thatch of dark curls surrounding it tempted her to slide her fingers through them.

"Anything wrong, Celine?"

Was he toying with her? He had to know he was a lot bigger than most men. She was wondering how in the world gigantic him would get into tight little her. There was no way she wouldn't be tight after not sharing any man's bed in almost four years. "Nothing is wrong as long as you promise to go easy on me."

He lifted a brow. "Go easy on you?"

OMG! Did he need her to spell it out for him? She would if doing so would spare her unnecessary physical pain later. "I haven't done this in almost four years."

She saw disbelief in his eyes. "You're kidding, right?"

"No, I'm not kidding, Zion."

"What about…?"

"All that stuff you've read and heard?" she offered. "Especially how I jet-set all over the world with my numerous lovers?"

"Pretty much," he muttered in reply.

She shook her head. Most of the time when the tabloids were accusing her of those things, she was hiding out in her office at Second Chances or behind the scenes at one of her soup kitchens. "I once warned you not to believe everything you read about me," she said, placing her hands on her hips, ignoring the fact that she was naked and he was getting an eyeful of her, like she was getting of him. "I've told you the score, so what do you intend to do about it, Zion?"

He moved closer and swept her into his arms and then whispered, "I'll go easy."

* * *

Or die trying, Zion thought, placing her back on the
bed and then lying beside her. Totally naked, they faced
each other without saying anything. At that moment nothing needed to be said. The sexual chemistry surrounding
them said it all. He wanted her more than he'd ever wanted
a woman and he needed to be cautious moving forward.
She was the one woman he'd broken rules for when he'd
mixed business and pleasure while in LA. But now she
was on his turf and he wouldn't break any more.

He leaned forward and captured her lips in a demanding
and greedy kiss. Intentionally so. With his mouth clamped
to hers he took total possession. He knew the desire was
mutual when she moaned deep into his mouth. Then he
began touching her practically everywhere, loving the feel
of her velvety skin.

Zion suddenly broke off the kiss to stare down at her
and she tipped her head to stare back. At that moment,
something—he wasn't sure exactly what—happened. The
connection was like a click in his brain and he felt invis-
ible threads tighten between them. He resented the feeling
and in protest he cradled her face in his hands, claiming
her mouth again, boldly sweeping his tongue between her
parted lips.

He reluctantly released her mouth and eased from the
bed to grab his jeans off the floor. After opening his wallet, he pulled out a condom packet. He was very much
aware that Celine was watching attentively as he eased it
on. A part of him recalled what she'd said earlier about his
size. She wasn't the first woman who'd made reference to
it. However, it was the first time such a comment actually
mattered.

"Had you asked, I would have told you that I'm on the pill."

He glanced over to where she lay, propped on the bed

in one hell of a sexy pose. Just looking at her naked body made the blood in his veins burn hot and molten. "It would not have mattered," he said, coming back to the bed. "I wear a condom regardless."

"Another one of your rules?"

"Yes, another one of my rules. Like I told you, I am fiercely bound to them."

"Umm, one day you're liable to come unbound," she said.

"That will never happen."

Tired of talking, he pulled her into his arms and kissed her, loving the warm and silky feel of her mouth. For the past month she had been the one constant in his mind, the one person he'd thought about when he went to bed, the one and only to ever invade his dreams. And now she was here.

Zion could feel the air surrounding them suddenly take on a life of its own, becoming sexually heated with a nuance of desire so intense it seemed to overpower him, made him intensify the kiss even more. He was driven to touch her between her legs and stroke the swollen folds of her moist femininity.

This time she was the one who pulled back from the kiss, the one who cradled his face in her hands to whisper, "I want you inside me, Zion."

At that moment every single nerve in his body vibrated in both anticipation and need. "I want to be inside you, too."

He meant it with every ounce of his being. "I'm going to let you control things," he said, lifting her into his arms and placing her on top to straddle him. "This way you take inside you only as much of me as you want."

"I want it all."

He wanted her to have it all. "You can and will. Take your time. No rush." He just hoped he could keep control and handle the torture.

Zion stared up at her as his hard, solid erection poked against the folds of her warm womanly core. Just the thought that his engorged manhood was there at the entrance of her mound made sexual excitement curl in his stomach.

She grabbed hold of his shoulders as she stared down at him. "I hope you're ready for me, Zion."

He was more than ready. When she began lowering herself onto him, he gritted his teeth as bone-melting fire began spreading through his bloodstream. And at that moment all he could do was whisper her name with a need he couldn't hold back.

This was a first for Celine. Never had any man allowed her to do this, use this position to take control. But now Zion was giving her this chance to regulate their lovemaking. When the head of his erection began entering her, she could feel her body stretching to accommodate him. Their gazes locked in the process and she knew from the way he was gritting his teeth that he was fighting the urge to thrust up hard inside her.

As she'd known it would be, her body was tight. She kept lowering herself onto him and his hardness seemed to fill every inch of her, until she couldn't press down any farther.

"Hold still for a moment," he whispered. "You've accomplished a lot already."

Had she? He wasn't even halfway inside her. "Open your legs a little wider," he instructed in a soft yet husky tone.

Celine did so and then gave a satisfied sigh when she felt herself sinking even farther, taking more of him inside.

When she knew he was embedded as deep as he could possibly go, she lowered her head and met his lips. The kiss they shared was hot and carnal. Feeling totally exhilarated, she began moving, slowly. Then she picked up speed, moving to her own rhythm, and began riding him.

The lower part of her pelvis moved up and down and she loved the feel of him fitting so snugly inside her.

She broke off the kiss and whispered against his moist lips, "I want you to take over now, Zion. And please take me hard."

She didn't have to make the request twice. Without missing a beat, Zion quickly switched their positions so that he was on top. The moment she was pinned in place beneath him, he began thrusting in and out of her, withdrawing and then reentering her again. Over and over. Her fingers dug deep into his shoulder blades, but he felt no pain. What he felt was pleasure so intense, so toe-curling, so fantastic, that he was driven to lean down and cover her mouth with his own again. He kissed her while his body took hers the way she'd asked him to, appeasing the sexual hunger neither of them could contain any longer.

Celine's inner muscles were gripping him, holding him, milking him for the semen the condom prevented him from sharing with any woman. But damn, he enjoyed the feel of her trying. When her body arched upward to receive his thrusts, he couldn't ever remember experiencing this feeling with any other lover. He was burning, on fire, and the flames threatened to consume him.

With one last thrust he was pushed over the edge, the same time she was. Simultaneously, screams tore from their mouths.

"Zion!"

"Celine!"

Sensations ripped through him, spiraling him into one hell of an orgasmic explosion. Throwing his head back, Zion screamed out his pleasure in a way he'd never done before.

The need to kiss her again consumed him, urging him

to connect with her mouth just as another orgasm slammed into him. He captured her lips, sucking them into his mouth with a need that pulsated in his very soul.

Moments later, when his body ceased its vibrations and his breathing returned to normal, he eased off Celine and pulled her against him. Instinctively, her body curled into him and he wrapped himself around her. Loving the feel of her in his arms.

Chapter 16

Hours later, unable to sleep, Zion eased from his bed and pulled on his jeans. He glanced at the wall clock and saw it was almost three in the morning. After he and Celine had made love twice, they had gone downstairs to eat the pot-pie she'd cooked for dinner. The meal had been delicious and he'd surprised himself with a second helping. After dinner they had cleaned up the kitchen before returning to bed for another round of lovemaking, and had drifted off to sleep afterward.

He'd awakened before midnight to find her wrapped in his arms and their limbs entwined. Leaving her alone in that bed had been hard, but after unraveling their bodies, he had eased from the bed, re-dressed and headed for the door, with the intent of not looking back.

But he had.

Doing so had been his downfall. She'd been sleeping peacefully, with her face to him, and even while sleeping, she was beautiful. He loved her lips even more now that he'd spent an entire night tasting them. They were full, inviting, and he'd enjoyed devouring them time and time again. His gaze had drifted to the rest of her and he could make out her shapely body beneath the bedcovers. A body he'd enjoyed making love to. Too damn much. It had taken every ounce of his control not to return to that bed, but to walk out the door and go to his own room.

And he hadn't been able to sleep.

After making love to Celine he should feel totally and completely satisfied. Instead he felt restless and agitated, with a desire to rejoin her in that bed and break one more of his rules. Damn. Hadn't he broken a couple already because of her? There had been the business-versus-pleasure rule in Los Angeles, when he'd crossed the line and kissed her. And her being here, in this particular house, was breaking another rule. He tried convincing himself that with the kidnappers on her tail, her being here couldn't be helped. But that had nothing to do with the fact he'd gone to bed with her. That was not only a rule breaker but a game changer.

And now, hours later, he was having withdrawal. He wanted her again. However, that wouldn't be happening. He was determined not to break any more Zion's Rules, which was why she was in the guest room and he was here in his own bedroom. Regardless of the fact he was feeling restless and agitated. Namely because other than those sexual desires eating at him, he had a strong feeling there was more to Celine than her beauty, curvaceous body and gorgeous legs.

He had figured that out over dinner, when the conversation somehow shifted to the state of the economy, world and domestic affairs and politics. It was obvious she was well versed on a number of topics and had strong opinions about particular ones. And they'd been opinions she hadn't minded expressing. He liked that about her—her ability to speak her mind and have no qualms about doing so. At first, in LA, her outspokenness had bothered him, but now he saw it was just a part of who she was.

He moved to his bed again and, lifting the covers, eased back inside. Why did it suddenly feel cold and empty when it never had before? He knew his desire for one particular woman was messing with his mind, but he refused to go there. What he needed to do was get his rest, in order to deal with what he anticipated would be Celine's attitude tomorrow. He figured that, like most women, she would not like that he'd left her bed without staying the entire night. Women expected to be held and cuddled after sex, but that wasn't part of his makeup, so he'd made it one of his rules. He would tell her that, and if she didn't like it, then it would be her problem, not his.

Celine opened her eyes, not sure what had awakened her. Maybe it was the sound of something stirring outside the window. Hopefully only a wild animal, she told herself, recalling what Zion had told her about being safe here. Besides, no one knew where she was and who she was with.

She flipped over on her back and stared up at the ceiling, not surprised she was in this bed alone. She had expected such a move from Zion. It was obvious the man had commitment phobias, and that was his issue, not hers. Yet she couldn't help wondering why.

Celine shifted again to glance over at the clock on the nightstand. It was hard to believe it was almost four in the morning. She drew in a deep breath and inhaled Zion's masculine scent lingering in the bedcovers.

She closed her eyes and remembered all she and Zion had done in this bed. Every single detail. Yet, even after all that, there was a degree of restlessness consuming her. Either that or after a few rounds of sex, she'd gotten addicted to Zion Blackstone. She'd never gotten addicted to anything in her life, so such a thing had to be impossible. Besides, Zion was a complicated man and she preferred not dealing with any more complications right now. She had enough to contend with.

Tomorrow would be a new day and she would make the best of it. The last thing she intended to do was make Zion think she was one of those needy women like that Bettina, who'd called a third time last night. They had been eating dinner, and when Celine asked Zion if he intended to take the call, he'd given her a firm no. For a quick minute she had felt a little bit of sympathy for the pesky Bettina, then just as quickly recalled the woman's attitude toward her. The bitchiness and jealousy hadn't been warranted. Who got possessive over a man who evidently didn't want you? Or a man who had no intention of taking an involvement with you seriously? Celine was not that kind of woman and figured Zion would quickly figure that out.

Satisfied with those thoughts, Celine closed her eyes and went back to sleep.

"Good morning, Zion. You're up early."

Zion turned from the stove and braced himself for Celine's fury at being left alone in bed. "Since you cooked dinner last night, I figured I would tackle breakfast."

"Oh, aren't you sweet."

Sweet? He'd been called a lot of things by a woman the morning after, but *sweet* wasn't one of them.

"So, what do you have planned today?" she asked.

"I'm working on a few pieces at the cottage, but I will take a break around lunch. If the weather holds I thought I'd show you the way down to the lake. You might like it there."

"That would be nice. Thanks."

"And if you're ready to eat now I'll put everything on the table," he said.

"Yes, I'm ready. I have a ferocious appetite this morning."

"Do you?" he asked.

"Yes. Do you need help with anything?"

He shook his head. "No, I got this," he said, placing various platters in the center of the table. He'd cooked eggs, bacon and waffles.

"Mmm, everything looks good. Who taught you how to cook?" she asked.

He glanced at her as he took the chair across the table. "When I first moved to Rome I was living on a limited budget. I made my jewelry by day and moonlighted as a waiter in this restaurant. One day the cook got mad and walked out, and since the owner thought I was the one with the most promise, he threw me in the kitchen and taught me what I needed to know as a breakfast cook. I worked there for two years, and by the time I left I was helping out with evening meals."

She nodded. "How did you become the former First Lady's jeweler?"

"By luck. Just so happens one of my regular breakfast customers was a good friend of the president. They attended Harvard together. He told him about me and Mr. President requested samples of my work. He liked what he saw and I was commissioned to design something for her birthday."

Celine smiled at him. "The world saw it and then every woman wanted jewelry by Zion. You became all the rave."

"It pays the bills," he said, trying hard not to stare at how she was licking syrup off her fork.

"Evidently. I love both your condo and this place."

He didn't say anything for a minute and then asked,

"What do you intend to do today? Unfortunately, there aren't any shopping malls close by."

She shrugged. "No problem. I've got my laptop with me. You have Wi-Fi here, right?"

Laptop? Why would she need a laptop? "Yes, I have Wi-Fi."

"Good. If you don't mind giving me the password I'll be all set."

For what? he wondered. And why hadn't she mentioned anything about their time in bed together? Wrapped in each other's arms. Connected to each other's body. Was she not upset that they hadn't spent the entire night together? That he had left her alone?

"How did you sleep last night?" he asked, refusing to let it go. Refusing to let her forget when he couldn't.

She smiled again as she piled more eggs onto her plate. "I slept like a baby. That bed was the bomb. I'm glad that's the bedroom you gave me to use."

He tried not to glare at her, but stared down at his plate as he began eating. Why was her nonchalant attitude pissing him off? He should be glad it hadn't bothered her that he'd left her bed after making love to her several times.

They ate in silence and were definitely not acting like two people who'd shared a bed hours ago. Two people who had scorched the sheets. He was programmed to act like he didn't give a damn—but what was her excuse? And did she have to sit there looking good enough to eat this morning? Beautiful as ever, with every strand of hair in place and her natural beauty almost taking his breath away? Hell, he bet she would look gorgeous even on a bad day. Even on a bad night. But she hadn't had a bad night. He thought it had been good. All good. Mind-blowing, earth-shattering good. So why wasn't she annoyed with him instead of being downright friendly?

"I know you want to get started on your work today, so don't worry about cleaning up the kitchen. I'll take care of it."

Was she trying to get rid of him? Rush him off? Why did the thought irritate the hell out of him? "Will you?"

"Yes."

"And you're sure it's okay?"

"Positive, Zion. That's the least I can do after all you did."

He lifted a brow. "All I did?"

"Yes. Breakfast is good."

"Thanks." He took a sip of his coffee as a stream of sensations flooded his stomach. Breakfast might be good, but what they'd shared in that bed last night had been over-the-top sensational. She might have pushed all the memories to the back of her mind, but he was determined that tonight, and all the nights that followed, she would never forget.

Chapter 17

Celine got up from the table to pour another cup of coffee. Glancing out the window, she saw it was dark, which made sense since it was close to ten at night. It was hard to believe this was her fourth day here.

Over the last couple of days she and Zion had established a comfortable routine. Every morning they shared a breakfast he prepared, and then he would leave to go work at the cottage. She used her free time during the day to research real estate for the future expansion of Second Chances. An additional facility to house more homeless individuals would be needed sooner rather than later.

Zion usually stopped for lunch and they prepared something together, often soup and sandwiches. He would return to work until around five in the evening. That gave her a chance to prepare dinner. She loved his kitchen and had found a recipe book with a number of dishes she'd tried.

She enjoyed the time they spent together. He'd told her more about his godbrothers and the women they'd married, as well as his godparents. Zion had even told her about the club that he and his five godbrothers had formed, the Bachelors in Demand Guarded Hearts Club, and the reason for doing so. It seemed at the time all six of them had been going through their own personal hell with women, and they'd made a pledge to remain single forever. Celine couldn't help but wonder what personal hell a woman had put Zion through.

He'd told her that all five of his godbrothers had married since then, leaving him the lone member of the club, but that he was determined to keep it going, no matter what.

Zion rarely spoke of his parents, and those times he did, she was the one who initiated the discussion. She knew his father, now retired, had been a sales executive at a company that sold medical equipment to hospitals, and his mother had been a nurse. Only because she'd asked, he had told her how his parents had met, but she hadn't been able to tell whether their marriage had been a happy one.

Celine had also shared information about herself. He hadn't asked her about her ex, Jerome, and she'd seen no reason to tell him. Nor had she mentioned anything about Second Chances. Instead she'd told him about her days at the university and about her friendship with Desha.

They would clean up the kitchen together and wind down their day by watching a movie in his theater room. Then they would retire, always using her bed in the guest room. He would make hot, blazing love to her, causing her to scream his name and behave wantonly between the sheets.

Celine would admit that she looked forward to her nights with him, when the sexual chemistry that had been building all day would reach the point of no return, and making love seemed the only way to get it stabilized.

Sex with him was always earth-shattering. She'd never experienced anything like it and doubted she would again with anyone else. She was sure that being made love to by Zion Blackstone was something she would sorely miss when she left here. Instead of counting the days till she could leave, she was wishing for a way to stop time.

Despite the pleasure he gave her each evening, she was very much aware that Zion never spent the entire night in her bed. He would leave around one or two in the morning and return to his own room. And he never invited her there. She had no idea how it even looked.

She tried not to let his actions bother her, but in a way they did, though not enough to make waves. She was aware of his rule. Still, deep down, she wished it could be different.

She also tried not to let it bother her that she hadn't heard from her father. She refused to call him, and for some reason he hadn't contacted her. She wanted to believe he was working with the authorities on making sure those men left her alone.

Her thoughts shifted back to Zion. She hadn't just imagined that his mood had changed today. He had been quiet at breakfast, when he was usually talkative. And he hadn't returned for lunch. Instead, she'd gotten a text on his burner phone saying he'd decided to work through lunch and dinner and would fix something to eat at the cottage. Was he trying to avoid her? If so, why?

"What are you still doing up, Celine?"

She glanced up, and when she saw Zion standing there, her heart began beating a little faster. Had he hoped she wouldn't be around? Usually she was in bed by now... with him.

He stood there, leaning in the doorway and looking just as sexy as he had that morning. Maybe even sexier.

She loved a man who wore jeans that looked as if they

were made just for him. And his shirt had the top two buttons undone, giving him a manly look. Too much of one.

She couldn't help studying his features, ones she'd thought about all day. Ones that could rattle her brain. Was she imagining it or were his eyes more intense than they had been that morning?

She released a frustrated sigh, knowing she had missed seeing him today. Had missed spending time with him. And why was she beginning to feel his absence today had been deliberate and he was trying to avoid her?

Why couldn't she just answer his question and be done with it, instead of standing there like a nitwit and appreciating every single inch of him? She knew doing so couldn't be helped. The man was so darn gorgeous. Chocolate eye candy of the most delicious kind.

"Any reason I should be in bed?" Suddenly, her mind conjured up plenty of reasons, and all of them included him. She tried to push out of her mind just what the two of them usually were doing at this time each night.

"I just figured you would be."

"I had a lot of work to do," she said, going to sit back down at the table holding her laptop.

"A lot to do like what?"

If only he knew. However, she had no reason to tell him. "It doesn't matter."

"I guess you've become an online shopper."

He still teased her about that, but tonight for some reason she was getting a little annoyed about it. Did he think that was all she did with her life? But then it occurred to her that he had no reason to think otherwise, and she'd told him no different. Wasn't that what she wanted everyone to assume? So she could go about doing her business at Second Chances without being under anyone's watchful eyes…especially those of her father? In a way, it didn't matter, since she planned to tell him the truth when she returned to the States.

"And why are you sitting here at the kitchen table working, when I have an office you could have used?" he asked, interrupting her thoughts.

She'd been using his office the other days and had enjoyed doing so, thanks to the fantastic view. But today after he'd texted and said he would be missing lunch and dinner, she'd brought her laptop into the kitchen. Doing so gave her a good view of his workplace. For some reason she'd felt closer to him in here. Why she'd needed that feeling, she wasn't sure.

"Any reason you changed clothes?"

So he had noticed she was wearing something different from this morning. That she had changed out of the jeans and top and was now wearing a sundress. It didn't matter that the outside temperature was rather cool. Around noon she had begun feeling hot. It probably had something to do with him being on her mind and her reliving the memories of all those nights in his arms. Whatever the reason, she'd felt the need to take a shower, and then she'd changed.

"No reason, other than I decided to make it a dress day. Jeans are okay, but I like wearing a dress every now and then," she said. There was no need to mention she had nothing on underneath. No bra or panties. Other than the material of the dress, she hadn't wanted anything else touching her skin…until he did.

"So what were you doing?" he asked, heading to the coffeepot.

Celine tried deciphering his mood, hoping it had improved since that morning. He was certainly full of questions, she thought, watching him cross the room and appreciating every step he took. Why did Zion Blackstone have to be so handsome, so powerfully built, with all those dreadlocks flowing around his shoulders? Why did he have to be a triple dose of masculinity on legs that could make a woman's hormones go crazy?

He glanced over and caught her staring, and she drew in a deep breath. Why had she been thinking about how his fine body had felt all over her, inside her?

"Celine?"

She blinked. "Yes?"

"So what were you doing all day?" he asked again, after pouring a cup of coffee.

She could tell him it was none of his business, but she was sick and tired of him thinking she was some irresponsible, jet-setting shopaholic with no direction in life. "I had several reports to do."

He lifted a brow. "Reports?"

She crossed her arms over her chest. "Yes, reports." And for now, that was all he needed to know.

Evidently, he didn't think so, for he asked, "What kind of reports?"

Celine was about to tell him it was none of his business when his cell phone rang. She watched him pull it out of his pocket and glance over at her. "I need to take this."

He then quickly walked out. Whoever was calling was evidently important. And she noted the call had come through his regular phone and not the burner. Was the caller a female?

What if it was? What if he'd reached out to that Bettina chick and given her his regular cell number and she was the one calling? Celine still had his burner phone and Bettina hadn't called once today. Was that why? And was that why his attitude had changed with her? Why he was trying to avoid her? Was Bettina back on the scene and Celine was cramping his style?

Her lips tightened to a frown and she tried to calm her

raging emotions and the jealousy she was beginning to feel. She drew in a deep breath, deciding to read over the report one more time before sending it to Stuart. And then she'd go to bed, knowing tonight, she would be doing so alone.

Zion went into his office and closed the door behind him. "Hold on for a minute, Y."

Zion put the phone down and drew in a deep breath. He had tried arranging it so he wouldn't see Celine today and hadn't counted on her still being up. She was becoming too much temptation for him. Way too much. He'd realized just how much when he found it harder and harder to leave her bed every night to return to his own. He had begun wondering how it would be to sleep through the night with her body plastered against him. How it would feel to not wear a condom while making love to her, to enjoy sex talks with her. To cuddle.

He'd discovered Celine was someone he could talk to easily, and had even thought about telling her about his mother's deathbed confession. Even thinking of sharing something like that with her crossed the line, and he knew immediately he needed to put distance between them while she was here. Baring his soul to any woman was something he simply refused to do.

It was funny how he'd gone through life dating when it suited him and not getting caught up in any woman. They'd been there for his enjoyment, and he had no problem thinking he'd been there for theirs, too. When the fun time was over, he went his way and they went theirs. And there definitely had never been a woman he'd spent nights thinking about.

Until he'd met Celine.

Hell, he'd even spent today thinking about her, and hadn't been able to get much work done. Out of sight and out of mind hadn't worked for him today where she was concerned.

Drawing in another deep breath, he put the phone back to his ear. "Thanks for holding on, Y. You got something?"

"Yes, I got something."

Zion's forehead crinkled. "What?"

"First of all, I contacted Alessandro to get a make on those guys who'd been casing the hotel, waiting for Ms. Michaels to return. They finally left after day one, but by then I had my men in place to keep them within their scope, to see if perhaps others are involved. The tail is going to cost you."

Rolling his eyes, Zion said, "Whatever."

"Boy, you're an easy client. Maybe I should double my price."

Zion shook his head. "What else is there, Y?"

"Did you know Celine Michaels had a personal body double?"

"A body double? No. Why would she need a body double when she's not a full-time actress? She mentioned doing a couple of movies her father produced a few years ago, but she never caught the acting bug." Zion was well aware that actors often used body doubles as stand-ins during stunts and nude scenes.

"That's what I intend to find out. It seems she uses one quite frequently to give the impression she's in a particular place when she's not. Earlier this year she was supposed to be in the Canary Islands for three weeks and her body double was there instead. The same thing happened four other times this year in other places. That makes me wonder where she is when she uses her body double."

Zion frowned. "You're sure about this?"

"Positive. I was watching videos of her last few trips abroad to see if perhaps I noticed the same faces in a crowd or something. I didn't. But I did notice that although the body double is a dead ringer for Ms. Michaels from a distance, a facial scan indicates a different person. Is she living a double life for some reason?"

Now, that was a good question, one Zion didn't have the answer to. "Is her body double working for her somewhere now?"

"No. It shouldn't be difficult to find out the identity of the other woman if we need it. She's probably the same woman who was her body double when she starred in movies a couple of times."

Zion didn't say anything, but he would admit to uploading both movies to his phone a few weeks ago. Late one night when she'd been on his mind, he had watched them back to back. Both were thrillers and he'd thought her acting had been pretty damn good.

"I'd like to know why she still uses the woman on occasion and if it has anything to do with what's happening in Italy. What if she's connected to whatever Nikon Anastas is mixed up in a lot more than what she's telling you?"

Yes, what if...

Zion found a number of ideas going through his head. Ideas he didn't want to consider, but knew he had to. What if Celine was involved and was using him as some sort of decoy? Using that body double had definitely shown she was a woman who couldn't be trusted. Just like his own mother had been. Cold chills ran through him at the thought.

"I don't know why she would have a body double that she uses frequently, Y," Zion said. "But you better believe I intend to find out."

"And there's something else. Something just as important."

"What?"

"Just as we thought. Levy Michaels lied. He hasn't re-ported any kidnapping of his daughter to the FBI."

Zion released a frustrated breath. "Why do you think he lied about that?"

"I don't know. Michaels and Anastas are up to some-thing and I'm determined to find out what."

And Zion intended to find out if Celine was somehow mixed up in it and playing him for a fool.

"We need to talk."

Celine looked up from her computer to find Zion stand-ing in the doorway, his arms crossed over his chest. She could feel anger radiating off him and wondered why. If the caller had been Bettina she'd probably told him Celine had hung up on her yesterday. As far as Celine was con-cerned, the woman had deserved it. Celine had refused to listen to any more garbage the woman might spew dur-ing her jealousy fit.

"I need to finish this report. We can talk tomorrow."

She could tell by the way his jaw tightened that he hadn't liked that suggestion. That was too bad. She was not in the mood. She was mad at herself for thinking about him most of the day and mad at him for getting into her thoughts in the first place. She knew it sounded crazy, outright ridicu-lous, but at the moment she didn't care. If he could have his mood swings then she could certainly have hers.

"Oh, you're wrong. We are talking tonight. I want to know why you have a body double who you use quite fre-quently, especially when you're jet-setting around the world."

How did he know that? Now she was the one glaring. "How do you know about Tiffany?"

"It doesn't matter how I know. I want to know why she's being used."

It did matter how he knew. Whoever had called him

evidently had told him something. Who? "I'm not telling you anything."

He moved away from the door and began strolling toward her in a way that was both menacingly sexy and uncompromisingly dangerous at the same time. She had the good sense to save her document, feeling a confrontation coming on.

He came to a stop at the table and she tilted her head back to stare up at him.

"Wrong, Celine. You showed up at my place at two in the morning, claiming someone tried to kidnap you—"

"Someone did try to kidnap me," she said, interrupting his tirade. But he ignored her and kept talking.

"Foolish me, I offered you my protection without checking things out first. Glad I decided to do so anyway. Now I'm suspecting you're up to something, and whatever it is, you're using a body double as a cover-up. That makes me think there's more to your kidnapping than you're letting on."

"What?" she said, trying to follow his train of thought. Did he think her occasional use of Tiffany to fake her whereabouts had something to do with her kidnapping? The possibility that he did pissed her off and she angrily stood up from her chair. Evidently he saw the fire in her eyes and had the good sense to take a step back.

"My getting kidnapped has nothing to do with Tiffany, you ass. How dare you insinuate such a thing?"

"Ass? I brought you here to protect yours. Now I discover you've been hiding stuff from me."

"And it was *stuff* that has no bearing on the danger I'm in," she snapped.

"Let me be the judge of that."

Celine's glare darkened and she placed her hands on her hips. She wouldn't let him be the judge of anything.

There was no reason she couldn't level with him and tell him why she'd needed Tiffany, yet for him to question her character was pretty damn low. "I'll let you be the judge of nothing, because I'm not telling you one single thing."

She tried to sidle past him and leave the room, but he reached out and grabbed her arm. The moment he did so, instead of her anger igniting even more, she felt intense fire of the most sexual kind. She could tell from the concentrated heat in his eyes that he felt it, too. Suddenly, she was driven to act in an insane way. In a second of sheer madness, she reached out and ripped off his shirt, sending buttons flying everywhere.

Shock replaced the heat in his gaze. Before she could back up, he reached out and countered her attack by ripping the dress off her, leaving her totally naked. His eyes raked every square inch of her bare body, and in their path, desire ignited her flesh. Driven by total sexual awareness, she threw her arms around his neck just as he lowered his mouth to hers.

After that, she wasn't sure what happened. It was like something exploded within both of them. She didn't know how he managed to shed his pants and boxers so quickly, but he did. And then he lifted her up in his arms and she automatically wrapped her legs around him as he backed her against the kitchen wall while devouring her mouth.

She felt the huge head of his erection pressing into her and was about to break off the kiss and remind him of what he'd told her. That he never made love to a woman without a condom. Evidently he was too far gone to realize he was doing just that.

Instead he held tight to her thighs, widened them as he continued to push hard and deep inside her. She felt herself being stretched inch by delicious inch and loving every minute of it. Then he began moving, thrusting deep, banging hard. Each stroke seemed to touch her very core, to permeate the very air they were breathing with the scent of bodies mating relentlessly. Why did he have to feel so good?

She wondered if he would let up and hoped and prayed that he didn't. Not when he sent desire pulsing through her with every thrust. She held him tighter, devouring his mouth in the same greedy way he was devouring hers.

Then he broke off the kiss and threw his head back with a guttural groan, and at the sound her entire body lit up, ready to explode. She was caught up in a carnal need so intense that a surge of yearning overtook her. And then suddenly she felt him, the hot semen that shot into her, making her aware of what he'd done and how much she liked the feel of him doing it.

A low moan slipped past her lips and her muscles began milking him for more, not caring how she was sizzling inside. He gave a deep, hard thrust and the feeling triggered an explosion that ripped all the way through her, making her scream his name. "Zion!"

Then he took her mouth again, kissing her like he was savoring her taste while he continued to pump hard inside her, filling her with even more of his molten liquid. It was as if he'd been saving it just for now. Just for her.

When he broke off the kiss to throw his head back and groan yet again, she buried her face in the hollow of his throat as if she needed to breathe in his scent. And then she felt the need to do something else. She sucked on his skin, leaving her mark. A mark made by Celine.

It seemed he knew the moment she'd done so, and he looked at her. The dark heat in his eyes was hot and sharp, and it pushed her to make her inner muscles clench him with a greed she knew he could feel. And when those same inner muscles began milking him again, he gripped her tight and, without disconnecting their bodies, moved her from against the wall and over to the breakfast bar. After placing her on it, he began thrusting hard and deep inside again. It was as if he couldn't get enough.

And neither could she.

Zion slowly opened his eyes and glanced over at the clock on the nightstand. It was close to two in the morning. He and Celine had been mating like damn rabbits for the past three hours. The first thought that struck him was that he hadn't used a condom. Even when he'd realized his mistake he hadn't tried to correct it. Being inside her, skin to skin, had felt so damn good, and all he wanted to do was continue to make love to her that way. Had he lost his ever-loving mind? He had gone in to confront her about the information York had told him and they'd ended up ripping off each other's clothes instead.

She hadn't been wearing anything under that dress. Not a stitch. He had suspected she hadn't had on a bra, but he'd had no idea she hadn't been wearing any panties. Ripping off his shirt had been her first mistake and seeing her without any clothes had been his. Memories of their nights together had consumed him all day, and when he'd seen her naked, he'd been driven by desire so powerful he had surrendered without putting up so much as a fight. He had broken yet another rule with Celine Michaels.

At least when he'd finally brought her upstairs, he'd had the good sense not to take her to his bed, but back in this guest room again. He intended on leaving and going to his room; however, he still needed answers and was determined to get them. When she stirred he knew it was time he woke her up. Then he decided he wouldn't wake her just yet. He wanted to chill a moment and try to figure out why she, of all people, had managed to get under his skin.

Zion wasn't sure how long he'd lain there staring at her when she finally opened her eyes and looked at him. Before she could say anything, he said, "I want an answer to what I asked you earlier, Celine. Why are you using a body double?"

Chapter 18

Celine stared up at Zion. Just seeing him made sexual need stir to life inside her again. Would it ever let up? Would she always feel that robust surge of energy pass between them, making her want to be taken by him, over and over?

"Why can't you answer my question?"

His words put a temporary hold on her sexual needs as she dealt with her mental ones. She would answer his question, but first she had one of her own. "You had me investigated?"

Tonight he had questioned her character. How could he do that? He'd been there when she'd phoned her father. She had even let him listen in on the call, so how could he think such a thing?

"I didn't have you investigated, Celine. It's your father and Nikon Anastas I'm suspicious of. I questioned some of the things your father was telling you. First of all, why is he protecting Anastas?"

Celine had wondered the same thing. But then, she knew

her father. She believed he must be connected to Anastas in some way that any bad publicity attached to the man might cause Levy financial hardship. Her father liked basking in publicity as much as he enjoyed making money.

"So, you had my father and Nikon investigated?"

"Let's just say York is checking out their story for me."

He'd told her about his godbrother York Ellis, the ex-cop who was now a security expert. "That was him who called you?"

"Yes. In checking out information on your father and Anastas, since York believes in being thorough, he decided to check you out, as well. That's how he found out about the body double. He also discovered your father lied about bringing in the FBI."

Celine thought for the man to have discovered that she used a body double, he must be *very* thorough.

For the time being she wanted to just focus on what Zion had said about her father and the FBI. But from the way Zion was looking at her, she knew he was questioning her role in all this and wondering if she was as innocent as she claimed. She knew that was what needed to be cleared up first.

"Since I was a junior in college, I've been operating a business I didn't want my father to find out about, Zion."

His gaze flickered somewhat. "What kind of business?"

Instead of answering him, she sat up in bed, reached over and pulled out the top drawer of the nightstand, and retrieved the folder she'd placed there. She handed it to him. "This business."

He sat up in turn and began browsing through it. What she'd given him was a packet containing brochures of Second Chances services. The packet her marketing department had created to attract potential donors.

Moments later he glanced back at her with what looked

like both shock and admiration on his face. "This is your company?"

She nodded. "Yes, my brainchild. I started the company with trust funds I inherited from grandparents on both sides. Later I kept it replenished with the allowances my father enjoyed giving me. Don't get me wrong—Dad gives to a number of charities, but he doesn't believe in being a 'bleeding heart,' as he calls anyone who wants to do more. I happen to be one of those persons."

She paused a moment before continuing. "Instead of arguing with him about it, I've kept my work a secret from him. Even going so far as to hire a body double and make him believe all I wanted to do with my time was shop and jet-set all over the world. When he thinks that's what I'm doing, I'm usually planted right there in LA and working out of my office downtown."

Zion handed the folder back to her. "So all the stuff the tabloids print about you isn't true."

"I told you, more than once, it wasn't."

"But why go to that extreme, Celine? You'll be twenty-five in a few months. Why would a grown-ass woman sneak around and do something that's evidently your passion? Why are you afraid to tell your father about the good you're doing? Why are you allowing him to think he's manipulating you?"

Celine looked away for a second and then back at him. "Losing my mother was hard on me. If you recall, Dad mentioned at dinner your first night in LA how after Mom died we lived here in Rome for a while."

She paused a moment and then said, "The reason we did so was because the loss of my mother was so great I became grief stricken. I was only twelve and quite close to my mom. And I went into what doctors refer to as a sort of grief-driven mental shock, where for six months I couldn't talk. The doctors suggested I needed stability for a while and plenty of attention. After the therapist helped me work through it and I got my voice back, I recall him telling Dad the same thing could happen again if I lost someone else that I loved or was attached to."

"Namely him?" Zion asked.

"Yes. Namely him. While I was in college my father had a cancer scare. I almost lost him and that's all I could think about. Since then I've tried not to upset my father about anything, and over the years he's taken advantage of it."

"Like allowing him to link you and Anastas in a relationship for a publicity stunt?"

"Yes. And even persuading me to star in those two movies, although I hated doing so. Only good thing that came from that was meeting and becoming good friends with Tiffany Sorrell, the person used both times as my body double."

Zion nodded. "When you told me you'd been working on reports today, you were doing so for your company?"

"Yes. We had an important business meeting this week, which I needed to be back in LA for. Now, because of those kidnappers, I'm still here in Italy. I want them to conduct the meeting without me, which is the reason I worked on that report all day." At least she'd tried to work on it. Typically, such a report would not have taken her more than a few hours, but her mind had kept wandering with thoughts of Zion.

She rubbed a hand down her face. "Tiffany has nothing to do with what's going on with Dad and Nikon. I hire her whenever I want my whereabouts feigned. And if Dad hasn't involved the FBI in my kidnapping like he claimed to have done, then I want to know why he lied to me."

Zion wanted to know that, as well, and he knew York would discover the truth and provide the answers. In the meantime, there was another subject he needed to address with her. Namely, another rule he'd broken. In all his thirty-three years he had never made love to a woman without a condom, but he'd made love to Celine without one tonight. Several times.

There was no excuse for what he'd done. And what made things so horrific was that he had enjoyed it. He should have pulled out of her the moment he'd realized what he was doing. Instead, he'd gotten even more caught up in an ecstasy the likes of which he'd never experienced before.

"We need to talk about what happened between us, Celine." In a way, bringing up such a thing seemed odd when they were still naked and in bed together.

She met his gaze. "What about it?"

Did she really need to ask him that when she knew the answer? "I didn't use a condom."

"I told you I was on the pill, but it was your rule to use a condom anyway."

Yes, it was his rule. At least it had been. "It's always better to be doubly safe."

She frowned. "Do you think I would intentionally get pregnant from you? Is that what this is about, Zion?"

"I didn't say you would intentionally get pregnant, but there's a chance you could." *You could* be *pregnant.*

She studied him for a moment and he had a feeling he wasn't going to like what she had to say. She proved him right. "You don't like kids that much that you're afraid of having one of your own?"

Zion didn't say anything at first, tempted to let her think whatever she wanted. But for some reason he felt inclined to set the record straight. "I love kids, but I don't plan to father one if I can help it."

"Why?"

Celine had no right to ask him that, since it was none of her business. But then, it could very well be her business if she ended up pregnant. Women on the pill were known to get pregnant. Nothing was 100 percent safe.

She was looking at him, waiting for a response. How could he explain that not knowing if Langren Blackstone was his biological father had a major impact on him? How could Zion bring a child into the world when he wasn't certain of his own parentage? There was no way he would tell Celine the true reason he'd turned his back on extending the Blackstone line and why he was willing to let it end with him. The last remaining Blackstone. So instead he said, "Fatherhood doesn't agree with me."

"I'll remember that in a month if I'm forced to do a pregnancy test."

He frowned and held her gaze. "I hope that doesn't happen, but if it does, I want you to know that I will accept my responsibility."

He knew what he said sounded cold and distant, but there was no hope for it. If she was pregnant he would want her to have the baby and he would do right by it.

"If I am pregnant, which I doubt, I don't need you to accept anything. I will take care of myself and my baby without you."

That wouldn't be happening but he decided not to argue with her. Instead he thought it best if he got out of her bed and got to his, where he belonged.

"So what's next…regarding my father? Do you think I should call and confront him about the FBI?"

Zion shook his head. "No, I wouldn't just yet. You have a place here where you are safe, and he has no idea where you are. I suggest you see how things play out with him while York continues his investigation. I would hope, whatever is going on, that your father has your best interests in mind."

"I hope so, too."

He glanced at the clock on the nightstand. It was time to go to his own bed. Returning his attention to her, he said, "Thanks for leveling with me about Second Chances, Celine. I think it's wonderful for you to care about others so much."

"Thank you."

"And another thing…" He forged ahead. "I think what you're doing is something you should be proud of and not keep hidden. I would think regardless of how your father feels about 'bleeding hearts,' that he would be supportive and proud of what you're doing."

She didn't say anything, just broke eye contact with him and stared down at the bed coverings for what seemed like a long moment before lifting her gaze back to him. "Thank you for saying that. For believing that."

Did that mean she didn't believe it? Thinking that was too much to dwell on at this hour, he said, "I need to go to my room."

"All right."

As if his hand had a mind of its own, he reached up and brushed his fingers against her cheek in an unexpected display of tenderness. "Chances are you won't be seeing me until late tomorrow again," he said huskily. "I have a lot to do to finish up that project I'm working on."

"I understand."

He wondered if she really did. Was she aware he would intentionally be putting distance between them again? He removed his hand from her face. Celine Michaels was too much temptation. For him to be in her bed now was confirmation of that. Once again she was testing his control.

He moved to ease from the bed, but his legs rubbed

against hers in the process. It was like a torch lighting dry kindling; immediately he felt a tightening low in his gut and every nerve in his body convulsed in sexual need.

Their gazes locked and held for the longest time. Then they began leaning toward each other, and within seconds were in each other's arms. The moment his tongue entered her mouth and she intercepted it, began feasting on it greedily, sexual excitement curled in his stomach. And he knew before he left her bed she would be rocking his world yet again.

Just like he intended to rock hers.

Chapter 19

Celine slowly opened her eyes and squinted against the bright sun shining through the windows. She shifted in bed to lie on her back and gaze up at the ceiling, but not before noticing the time was close to noon. It was hard to believe she'd slept this late, but then, maybe not.

Evidently intent on not breaking another rule, Zion had left her bed around three this morning, leaving her with a toe-curling kiss after hours of nonstop lovemaking. Lovemaking that had been so remarkable, her body was still tingling in aftershocks.

She closed her eyes, reclaiming last night's memories, recalling the moments after their lovemaking when she'd settled in his arms with her cheek pressed against his chest, listening to his heartbeat while her body hummed in absolute pleasure.

Even after Zion's spiel about the risk of a pregnancy because he hadn't worn a condom, he'd made love to her again—twice—without one. Then he'd left her bed. She'd known the exact moment he'd left, not to return. She would have felt a total sense of loss if he hadn't left her so totally and completely satisfied. The nights spent in his arms had been so fulfilling, so invigorating and exhilarating. She'd made love to Jerome just a few times, and she'd thought nothing could surpass that. She'd been wrong. Zion was in a class all by himself. And the words he'd spoken to her about Second Chances had been uplifting. They had bolstered her confidence and her belief that she was doing the right thing. That her company was impacting lives in a positive way.

Sitting up in bed, she lifted her arms over her head to stretch her body, feeling wonderful. Today she intended to push her father and Nikon from her mind, any thoughts of what the two of them were mixed up in, and how she was unwittingly involved. They had no idea where she was and she intended to keep it that way. If her father called she would continue to assure him she was safe, and for now that was enough. She agreed to stay out of it and let York Ellis find out the truth.

Deciding it was time to start her day, she slid from the bed to go shower and dress. There was no doubt it would be lonely, with Zion hiding out yet again in his workplace. At least yesterday she'd had that report to keep her busy; today she really had nothing to do.

Glancing out the window, she was again taken by the beauty of the land on which Zion's country home sat. That was when she made up her mind to go outside and enjoy it. She might walk to the lake. Being an only child, she was used to entertaining herself, and today would be no different.

Zion shut down his equipment, leaned back on his workbench and sighed deeply as he glanced over at the clock. It was a couple of hours past noon. Somehow he'd finished the jewelry pieces he'd been commissioned to make for

Celine. He hoped when she saw them on her birthday she would be pleased.

He smiled, thinking how for the past five years she had successfully run a huge charitable organization right under the media's nose without anyone finding out. Good for her. People running the newspapers, television and tabloids thought they knew all about every celebrity's business, and Celine had successfully proved them wrong.

He stood and walked over to the window as he thought again about last night, convinced the taste of her was still in his mouth. He no longer wondered why Celine had such an effect on him, just accepted that she did. But at least he knew he had an effect on her, as well. Together they were an explosion just waiting to happen—and it happened each and every time their bodies joined.

Zion was about to turn from the window when movement below caught his attention. It was Celine, wearing a pair of jeans and a pullover sweater. She was walking toward the lake with a blanket tucked under her arm. It was a beautiful day outside and he couldn't blame her for wanting to enjoy it.

An idea suddenly popped into his head. He tried forcing it away, but couldn't. Moving from the window, he quickly went into the kitchen and opened the refrigerator to grab the sandwiches he'd made earlier for lunch, but hadn't taken the time to eat. He also grabbed bags of chips out of his snack tray and a bottle of wine and two glasses. Placing all of them in the wicker basket he kept in one of the cabinets, he headed for the door.

"I hope I can join you."

Celine lifted her head off the blanket and looked at Zion. Pulling herself up in a sitting position, she drew in a deep breath. "I thought you'd be busy all day," she said, recalling what he'd told her last night.

"I have to eat sometime, and I have enough to share," he replied, producing a picnic basket from behind his back.

She smiled. "I appreciate your generosity."

"I made turkey sandwiches this morning before leaving the house," he said, kneeling and placing the basket in front of her.

"And you have my favorite chips," she said, looking into the basket and pulling out a bag of barbecue-flavored ones.

He reached for the wineglasses, then proceeded to uncork the bottle and pour wine into them. "This comes from one of Italy's finest vineyards."

"I can't wait to taste it. You thought of everything," she said.

"I tried to."

"Hmm, maybe I should warn you that I missed breakfast. It was noon before I woke up today and I'm sort of hungry."

"Then eat up."

They ate for a while in silence. But that didn't stop her from appreciating his presence, inhaling his scent, getting flooded with full sexual awareness of him.

"You still haven't heard from your father?" he asked, taking a sip of his wine.

"No. If you need me to leave, I can check into a hotel."

A frustrated expression appeared on his face. "Any reason we're back to that again?"

She didn't say anything for a minute, then stated, "Bettina has been blowing up your phone today."

"Where's the phone now?"

Celine leaned over, pulled it out of her jeans pocket and handed it to him. Was he going to return Bettina's call? Right now, while Celine was sitting there? She watched him and saw what he did before handing the phone back to her. "You blocked her."

"Yes, I blocked any further calls from her. I told her from the beginning I don't do long-term relationships. I guess she's determined to make a liar out of me."

Celine figured it had nothing to do with making a liar out of him. It was about tempting him enough to break his rules. Celine had done so and wondered why this Bettina couldn't.

As if Zion had read her thoughts, he said, "She doesn't get to me the way you do, Celine."

The intensity of his gaze focused on her stirred her insides. "How do I get to you, Zion?"

"I think you know, since I've broken a few rules for you."

Yes, he had done that. "Your broken rules might be reason alone for me to leave," she said, finishing off her sandwich and taking another drink of her wine.

"I want you to stay."

She studied his features and felt a tingling in her stomach as she watched him bite into his sandwich and slowly chew. Why was the movement of his mouth a total turn-on? "Why do you want me to stay?"

He didn't answer right away, just finished his sandwich, followed by a sip of wine. "I like having you around."

And she liked being around him.

They finished their lunch and wine. He surprised her by stretching out on the blanket and then pulling her down with him. "Have you ever been made love to under the beauty of the sky, Celine?"

"No."

"Then share the experience with me." He lowered his mouth to hers and she knew exactly how their picnic would end.

Chapter 20

Around three in the morning Zion woke to the ringing of his phone. After making love to Celine on the blanket by the lake for the majority of the afternoon, he had come back here to work at the cottage instead of going to the main house. He knew he would be tempted to make love to her even more. And because of that he'd stayed in the bedroom at the cottage.

Recognizing the ringtone, he said, "This had better be good, Y."

"It's about Levy Michaels."

Zion pulled himself up in bed. "What about him?"

"It seems Michaels planned his daughter's kidnapping as part of a publicity stunt orchestrated by Anastas, which is why he hadn't gone to the FBI."

"What!"

"You heard me. The reason for her kidnapping had nothing to do with Nikon Anastas owing anyone money. He never owed anyone anything. The plan fell through when

Ms. Michaels got away. Those men were to hold her for a week, and they would get paid a huge sum of money for their troubles. News of her kidnapping would have made national headlines, with Michaels being portrayed as the concerned and upset father and then Nikon as the hero when he showed up in Italy to rescue Ms. Michaels."

Zion couldn't believe what he was hearing. "That's the craziest thing I've ever heard of."

"Yeah, but those Hollywood types will do anything to get their name in the spotlight. Unfortunately, a monkey wrench was thrown into the plans. Once those men grabbed Ms. Michaels they got greedy and decided they would make more money with a real kidnapping. They called Anastas and Michaels and told them of their change in plans. A faked kidnapping had turned into the real thing and a ransom was demanded. That's why Michaels told his daughter to go into hiding—because he knew those men were looking for her. He and Anastas tried to talk some sense into the men, and when that failed, they had no choice but to finally go to the FBI today and admit what they'd done."

Zion got out of bed, livid. "That was a crazy publicity stunt, which could have gotten Celine hurt."

"I think her dad realizes that now. I understand the FBI is working with Rome officials to find those men. I would help them out, since I've kept a tail on them since day one, but if I do, the authorities will wonder about my involvement, and I intend to keep you from being connected to all this BS."

"I appreciate that."

"I figured you would. More than likely Michaels will be calling his daughter to explain everything. Hopefully, he'll tell her the truth this time. I understand he wants her back home and has no idea where she is. He's not even sure if she's still in Rome. A part of me suspects he's really worried about her now, since he hasn't talked to her."

"He could have. She's been using my burner phone."

"Evidently he was worried about the calls being traced by those guys," York explained.

Zion slid into his jeans and walked over to the window. He could see the guest bedroom where Celine was staying from where he stood. Suddenly the lights in the bedroom came on. She still had his burner phone, so he wondered if she'd just gotten a call from her father.

"Z? You still there?"

"Yes, I'm still here. I need to go to Celine. I'll talk to you—"

"Go to her? Where is she?"

"Staying at the main house."

"Oh. And where are you staying?"

He was about to tell York that he asked too many questions. Instead he answered, "At the cottage."

"Any reason the two of you aren't under the same roof?"

"No reason that's any of your business. Bye, Y. I'll call you back later."

Zion clicked off the phone, slipped on his shoes and headed for the door.

"What are you saying, Dad?" Celine asked, easing out of bed after turning on the lamp. She could hardly believe what her father had just told her.

"I'm sorry, sweetheart. When Nikon came up with the idea it sounded like a good plan, to put our names out there for that project we'll be working on together the beginning of next year."

"So this was all a publicity stunt?" She could feel anger tightening her throat.

"But things didn't go the way we'd planned," her father said. "Those men were supposed to hold you for a few days and then let you go. Nikon and I would then announce to the authorities that you'd been kidnapped, and that we'd paid your ransom. It would have been a great news story about how Nikon and I saved the day and got you back home safely. The PR would have been unbelievably great. Only thing, those men got greedy and tried making the kidnapping the real thing. I am so glad you got away from them."

Celine didn't want to think what might have happened if she hadn't. "I can't believe you would do something like that. Put my life in danger."

"Like I told you, I honestly didn't think you'd be in danger. Nikon assured me you wouldn't be."

"And when I called and told you what happened, why didn't you contact the FBI like you claimed you'd done?" She detected her father's annoyance. He detested being questioned about anything. He'd told her what he'd wanted her to know and that should have been final. But not this time. Now she needed to know the truth.

"Because I thought Nikon and I could handle it, that we could talk some sense into those men to back off, but we couldn't. They were intent on getting more money out of us. They threatened to tear up Rome looking for you and when they found you there would be hell to pay. That's when I knew that I had to let the FBI know what was going on. Especially when I had no idea where you were. I still don't."

And she still had no intention of telling him. The story would break and the names of everyone involved would be publicized. It wouldn't be the story her father had wanted out there, but that was too bad.

That wasn't what she wanted for Zion. He didn't deserve an invasion of his privacy just for trying to protect her.

"When can I return to the States?" She didn't ask when she could return to the Michaels estate. More than ever she was determined to move out into her own place.

"You're free to return now. I've been notified that the Italian police have apprehended those men and they've been arrested. The FBI has agreed not to make a statement about anything, since you got away and no harm came to you."

"So in other words, no one will know what you and Nikon planned to do."

Her father hesitated for a moment, then said, "For now. There's a possibility those men who were arrested will talk, but we'll deal with that when and if it happens."

Celine could only shake her head. Did he think being kidnapped for even a short while hadn't been traumatic for her?

"By the way, your phone should be working again. And I plan to be with Ulysses when he flies in to get you."

"Don't bother, Dad. I'll get back to the States on my own."

"Celine, I *will* be coming to get you."

"No, Dad, you won't. I will call you when I get to the States."

"Celine, I know you're upset about all this, but I'll make it up to you. How does an unlimited shopping experience in the Canary Islands sound to you?"

He actually thought that her emotions could be bought! Rage roiled inside her. But then, hadn't his attempts to soothe her in the past been basically the same—throwing money at her? Instead of going shopping, she'd invested the money into Second Chances. But not this time. "I don't want to go shopping, Dad."

"Of course you do. By the way, the Roman authorities want to talk to you. They can't hold those men until you officially file charges against them, and that needs to be done within seventy-two hours."

"I'm not ready to talk to anyone yet. When I am, I will. Goodbye, Dad."

As soon as she clicked off the phone, she heard the light knock on the door and knew who it was. Slipping on her robe, she said, "Come in."

A shirtless Zion walked in. "Are you okay, Celine?"

The intensity of her attraction to him still mystified her. "Is there a reason I shouldn't be?" She didn't mean to sound flippant, but she couldn't help it. After making love to her all afternoon by the lake, he had walked her back here, and instead of staying, he had escaped to the cottage. He'd even had the audacity to text her to say he would spend the night there. Why did he keep making love to her and then rejecting her?

"I got a call from York and he told me what he'd found out."

"And I just got a call from my father. He told me everything. He also said the Roman officials picked up the men and I need to go to the authorities and press charges within seventy-two hours."

Zion nodded. "No problem. I will take you wherever you need to go tomorrow."

She shook her head. "I'd rather you didn't."

He frowned. "Why?"

"Because no one knows where I've been for the past few days and I'd prefer to keep you out of it. I know how you feel about being in the spotlight and wouldn't want your name connected to mine. Somehow Dad got the FBI to agree to keep the incident out of the papers in the States, but if those kidnappers decide to talk it won't make Dad or Nikon look good."

"When and if the truth gets out, people are going to wonder where you were hiding," Zion said.

"Let them. I'll refuse to tell them. Like I said, I don't want you involved."

He came to stand directly in front of her. "Too late. I'm already involved. And I think you should wait a couple of days before you leave, to make sure the authorities arrest everyone who's been implicated."

She saw nothing wrong with his suggestion. In fact, she thought it was a smart move. "All right. And when I return to the States things will be different."

"In what way?"

She began pacing, knowing he was watching her closely. But she needed to move around. Standing near him for too long a time filled her with too many memories. The heat and texture of his skin. His taste. How much she enjoyed making love to him. She would even admit that she had missed him being in her bed last night. The short time he would have been there.

"In what way, Celine?" he asked again.

She stopped pacing and looked at him. "First of all, I plan to tell my father how I feel about what he and Nikon did. Although Nikon might have suggested it, Dad went along with it. For him to think he could manipulate me to accept a pretended kidnapping was not okay. He didn't consider my feelings. It was all about what he and Nikon wanted."

"I'm sure he's regretting that decision."

"Yes, and in a way, I hold myself responsible for allowing him to think he could control me all these years. Although I fought back, I never fought back hard enough, for fear I would lose him. But that will change. I had already made up my mind to tell him about Second Chances.

I refuse to sneak around to do something that makes me happy, not any longer."

She began pacing again and then she stopped. "And I plan to move permanently into my own place."

"Do you?"

"Yes. And maybe one day, if you ever get the notion to visit me, I'll happily return your hospitality."

Zion didn't know what to say to that, although he knew he wouldn't be visiting her. When she left here and he'd had the jewelry for her birthday delivered to her father, that would be the end of his association with the Michaelses. Although deep down the thought bothered him, that was the way it would be. The way it had to be. Celine Michaels was becoming an ache and the only way to get rid of it was with time and distance.

He needed to make sure she understood there was no future of any kind for them. No visits. No phone calls. No nothing. When she left, all contact between them would end. "Visiting you is not an option, Celine. Not when there is this thing between us. I see you and I want you. I see your lips and I want to kiss you. I see your naked skin and I want to taste you. God knows I tried avoiding you and couldn't. I don't understand it, but for now I'm willing to accept it."

He paused a moment and then added, "But I need you to accept something, too. There can't and never will be anything between us. All we can ever have is this thing that neither of us can control. A part of me wished there could be more, but there can't. I won't let it. I'm a loner and intend to be a loner for the rest of my days, and I'm okay with that. All we will ever have is the now. I'm willing to accede to that. Are you?"

She didn't say anything. All they did was stare at each

other as if the impact of his words was clearly understood. He wasn't sure who moved first. One of them did. Maybe both at the same time. All he knew was that suddenly she was in his arms, and once he lowered his head toward hers, he was crushing her mouth with his and exerting a provocative degree of pressure to take the kiss deeper.

She moaned and the sound barely harnessed his control. There was just something about kissing this woman, holding her in his arms, breathing her scent, that elicited a degree of passion he'd never felt before.

He loved seducing her mouth while his hands tangled in her hair and his fingers caressed the nape of her neck. He growled low in his throat and took the kiss to an ever deeper level. Moments later, when the need to breathe became mandatory, he reluctantly dragged his mouth away.

But the fire she'd started now spread through his blood and burned in his loins. He felt a possessive streak rush through him. Drawing in a ragged breath, he tried getting control of his mind and senses, but couldn't. It hit him then that Celine Michaels was different from any woman he'd ever met. She was getting to him in ways other women never had. He had broken his rules for her.

And he wanted to break another one.

Zion convinced himself the reason he intended to break this particular rule was because pretty soon she would be leaving and he would need the memories. At night, while sleeping alone, he wanted to recall a time he had made love to her in his bed. Why that was important to him, he wasn't sure, and he didn't want to analyze it. It just was. He would accept that she would be leaving a lasting impression on him and there wasn't a damn thing he could do about it.

Ignoring her gasp of surprise, he swept her into his arms and left the room.

"Where are you taking me, Zion?"

He paused a moment to look down at her before leaning in to sprinkle kisses around her mouth. When he began walking again, he lifted his head, met her gaze and said, "My bed."

A part of Celine didn't want Zion to break another rule for her. One day he would analyze his actions and resent her for them, and she didn't want that. She never meant to disrupt his life or drive him to do things he would later regret.

Just as she never meant to fall in love with him.

But she had.

She realized that now and figured it was something she'd always known, but was, until that moment, unwilling to accept. After all, Zion had made it crystal clear that he didn't want any woman's love. He'd been hurt in a way from which he would never recover.

She glanced around when he placed her in the middle of his bed. This was the first time she'd seen his bedroom. He always kept the door closed, so she'd never gotten even a peek inside. Now she saw how huge the room was and how beautiful. The furnishings suited him. Massive and masculine. The bed was mega-large and when he'd placed her in it she felt the firm mattress.

Celine was about to tell him not to break another rule for her when he reached out and removed her robe and then quickly dispensed with her gown, before sliding off his jeans. Just looking at his body took her breath away, and caused a fluttering in her stomach and a wetness between her thighs. Even her nipples were growing firm before his eyes.

"I love how you respond to me," he said in a deep, husky voice, joining her on the huge bed.

As if she could control herself not to respond. And when

he leaned close to nuzzle the side of her neck, she let out a deep sigh. She was putty in his hands. And when his arms wrapped around her, she eased into them even more. "And I like the way you respond to me." She couldn't miss the opportunity to counter what he'd said.

He lowered his mouth and she thought he intended to kiss her again. Instead he trailed his lips and his tongue down the side of her face. The unexpected move caused sensual tingles to spread all over her body.

He didn't stop. It was as if his tongue was enjoying the taste of her skin, savoring it as it moved slowly down her neck. When he reached her throat, he planted an open-mouthed kiss there at the center, before sucking at the skin, as if branding her. The thought made heat surge through her.

His mouth was on the move again and she found herself seduced by the hot glide of his tongue over her chest. The moment he took a nipple into his mouth, she moaned as threads of desire wrapped around her. She tugged on his locks, and it seemed the more she tugged, the harder he sucked. The pressure caused an ache at the juncture of her legs.

Then he moved upward until his tantalizing breath was against her mouth. When he swiped his tongue across her lips she moaned again. Why was he torturing her? As if he read her mind, he said, "I want you in ways I've never wanted a woman, Celine. I want to do things to you that I don't normally do."

Things he didn't normally do? Before she could find her voice to ask what some of those things were, he sealed his lips over hers, ravishing her in a kiss that rocked her to the core. She was determined to return the kiss with similar greed. Their tongues tangled, dueled, scraped together and mated relentlessly.

She felt him easing her down in the warm bedcovers, and then suddenly, he broke off the kiss, lifted her legs over his shoulders and buried his head between her thighs.

Celine screamed the moment his silky, hot tongue slid inside her and proceeded to give her the same type of intense kiss he'd always given her mouth. His tongue was so hungry for her it took her breath away. This kiss was mindless. It was drugging. It was searing. She tipped her head back against the pillow and of their own accord her hips rose to plant themselves more solidly against his mouth.

Jerome had never made love to her this way, and her first experience with Zion was nearly driving her insane, making her moan deep in her throat. She heard herself call his name, but instead of stopping to answer her, he continued to stroke her with his tongue into sweet oblivion. It was as if at the moment he had a one-track mind, deliciously focused and concentrated on giving her one hell of a demanding kiss, right there. Whether he knew it or not, he was claiming her in a way she'd never been claimed, filling her with a passion she'd never possessed.

His tongue dived deeper inside her, and an orgasm struck her hard. She let out a scream that she was certain shook the rafters and raised the roof. It was only after the last spasm had ended that he pulled his mouth away and moved her legs off his shoulders.

Then he was straddling her. Her body arched and her thighs opened wide while he eased inside her, holding her gaze captive. Her body became taut with renewed pleasure when he began moving. Over and over he pounded hard into her, and at times she gasped out loud at the magnitude of the sensations threatening to overwhelm her. She could feel a climax on the horizon, building fast.

And then it happened again. To both of them at once. Pleasure swept her body and he threw his head back and hollered her name. The sound triggered even more sensations that bombarded her. She heard a ragged growl near her ear just seconds before Zion hungrily slammed his mouth over hers.

Moments later, he eased off her and nestled her in his arms, saying, "Now we sleep."

She lifted her eyes to his. "In here?"

He leaned over and placed a kiss on her lips. "Yes, in here. All night."

"All night?" she whispered, clearly not believing it.

Placing a leg over hers as if holding her captive, he whispered back, "All night."

Chapter 21

Zion stood looking out his living room window, but turned around when he heard Celine. She was wearing a pair of boots and a sweater dress. Her coat was thrown over her arm and her other hand clutched her luggage. Their time together had come to an end and she was leaving. He'd never had a problem telling a woman goodbye, so what was the issue with this one?

And he knew there was an issue. A major one. She'd been here only a week, but it was a week that would be etched in his memory forever. And during those seven days he had broken rules he'd sworn he would never break. Rules that had been the essence of his being. How was he going to recover from that?

How was he going to go back to the way things were before she'd invaded his life? Invaded his space? And now she was leaving. He would miss her. The last two nights had been extra-special. Having her in his bed all through the night and waking up with her in his arms had placed him on a plane he'd never reached before and doubted he ever would again.

He moved over to where she stood. "I wish you'd reconsider and let me take you to town."

She shook her head. "No, I've called a car and this way is best. But I want to ask you to do me a favor."

He smiled down at her. "What's the favor?"

She hesitated a moment before saying, "I don't know about the woman who broke your heart, Zion, but the pain is keeping you from ever loving another. At some point I hope you discover that what you have bottled up inside of you is wasted energy. And it's negative. Replace it with positive energy and then make it useful. That's the only way your heart will heal."

When a car horn sounded, she smiled up at him. "Seems like my ride has arrived. Take care of yourself, Zion."

He nodded. "And you take care of you." Leaning down, he captured her mouth in a kiss he would store in his memory forever.

"What do you mean, you're moving out?"

Celine glanced over at her father. Her plane had landed a few hours ago and her dad had been at the airport to pick her up. Now they were in his study and it was obvious he was not happy with how their conversation was going.

So far the media hadn't gotten wind of Levy and Nikon's plan of a fake kidnapping to boost the ratings of their star meters at her expense. She was grateful for that. Enough news would be made when she gave a public statement in a few days about her involvement with Second Chances. Leveling with her father was the first step.

"I'll be twenty-five in a few months. It's time I move out."

"If you're leaving because you're upset with me, then…"

"Yes, I am upset with you, but that's not why I'm moving out. Like I said, I'm almost twenty-five and it's time to get my own place," she told him. There was no need to add that she'd begun looking for a place on the internet while in Rome. She'd seen one that was in a good location and just what she thought she needed. After seeing it tomorrow, she would put down a deposit if she liked it, and move in.

"I'm asking you to reconsider moving out, especially now. The timing isn't right. There is a possibility that kidnapping Nikon and I orchestrated will hit the news, especially if those men who were charged decide to talk. The three of us—me, you and Nikon—need to present ourselves as a united front until things die down. That also means you'll need to present yourself as Nikon's fiancée."

"Absolutely not! I will not do such a thing, Dad. And if I'm ever asked, I'll tell the truth—that at no time was there ever an engagement between me and Nikon. Nothing you say or do will make me change my mind about moving out or making it clear I am not engaged to Nikon."

"Then that's unfortunate."

Celine watched as her father poured a drink of scotch from the decanter on his desk. She knew this move. Had seen it a thousand times. The drink was his reinforcement when he was intent on making her come around to his way of thinking. Such manipulations might have worked in the past, but they wouldn't this time.

"I've apologized to you about what happened in Rome, Celine. And when you see Nikon, he will be apologizing, as well. Although your relationship with him was for PR, I truly believe he cares for you. I wish you could have seen how upset he was when we realized what those men were up to."

"Spare me, Dad. The only person Nikon is concerned about is himself. As of today I am ending this farce about us even being a couple. I prefer not seeing him again."

She knew her father hadn't liked what she'd said. Too bad. She had meant every word of it. "Now if you will excuse me, I need to—"

"Ending your relationship with Nikon is your business. However, if you move out I will cut off your allowance," her father stated angrily. "Then how will you take care of yourself? You've squandered your trust funds and don't have a penny to your name. Did you not think I had ways of checking?"

Celine was certain he had, which was why she'd established a dummy bank account for his benefit. "Contrary to what you might think, Dad, I am not penniless. I guess now is a good time to give you this," she said, opening her satchel and pulling out a folder. The same one she'd shared with Zion. She handed it to him.

"What's this?" he asked, taking it and looking inside. Levy Michaels browsed through the brochures and then closed the folder and looked at her. "I've told you that I'm not donating to any of these places."

"Doesn't matter if you don't, since the trust funds I got and the allowance you gave me in college were used to start that foundation. Second Chances is a five-year-old nonprofit company and it's mine. Goodbye, Dad."

Celine then turned and walked out of the study.

Chapter 22

Zion glanced over at the clock. It was past midnight and here he was, prowling around his bedroom, unable to sleep. He should never have let Celine spend the night in his bed. Even after a week her scent was still everywhere. In his bedcovers. In his room. He'd thought the memories would be comforting, but he'd discovered they were torturing him.

The courier had come yesterday to pick up the package that would be hand-delivered to Levy Michaels's representative, who'd arrived at the airport that morning. Zion had spoken to Levy two days ago and the arrangements had been made. He had been tempted to ask about Celine, but hadn't. Nor had he turned on his television to see what was going on with her. And he hadn't gone anyplace tabloids were sold.

But he couldn't help wondering if she had stood her ground with her father or if she had gone back to being under his thumb. Was Nikon still claiming the two of them were engaged? And why on earth did Zion give a damn?

And why hadn't he been able to sleep for a week for thinking of her? Reliving their nights together. Their days. Even those looks they'd given each other when neither thought the other had noticed. The innocent touches, as well as the not-so-innocent ones.

And why had putting her in that private car that had come to pick her up a week ago been the hardest thing he'd ever done? They had kissed goodbye and it had taken the driver several honks of his horn to make them step out of each other's arms.

One thing he felt pretty good about was knowing that the same blood-burning desire that had consumed him while she'd been here had consumed her, as well. She hadn't denied it, nor had she tried fighting it. And at no time had she tried putting distance between them like he'd done. She had accepted it and had been willing to give him time to accept it, too. And she hadn't pushed him into anything. Even a night spent in his bed. It had been something he'd wanted to happen. Something he had needed to happen.

More than anything he couldn't forget their lovemaking. With Celine he had encountered emotions he'd never had to deal with before. Strong emotions. Overwhelming emotions. Emotions that even now were shaking him to the core.

Nor had he forgotten the words she'd spoken before leaving… *"I don't know about the woman who broke your heart, Zion, but the pain is keeping you from ever loving another. At some point I hope you discover that what you have bottled up inside of you is wasted energy. And it's negative. Replace it with positive energy and then make it useful. That's the only way your heart will heal."*

For years he hadn't wanted his heart to heal. But what about now? Had he met someone who'd made the healing possible? Someone who made him want to get rid of all that wasted energy? All the negativity?

Someone who gave him a reason to stop running?

For years he'd thought himself incapable of displaying such heartfelt emotions for a woman. But thanks to Celine he was now feeling them, whether he wanted to or not. And the feelings were deep, deeper than anything he'd ever felt before. Why was he willing to let it be wasted energy?

Suddenly, it occurred to him that the emotion he was feeling wasn't lust, as he'd assumed. It was something a lot more meaningful, stronger and more potent. Heat suddenly began engulfing him. Heat and something else. Emotions were bombarding him, fighting within him. Negative versus positive. Which one would he allow to win?

He drew in a deep breath while thinking he wanted Celine in a bad way, but not just sexually. There was pleasure and then there was an even deeper pleasure in knowing you could care enough for a woman to want to make a difference in your life and in hers.

It was hard to believe that he, of all people, the last member of the Guarded Hearts Club, was finally seeing what all his godbrothers had already seen. Love in all its splendorous colors. He'd discovered that there was indeed a woman out there who could make him look at things differently. A woman who made him totally aware, sensuously and otherwise, that he wasn't meant to be alone.

The bottom line was that he had fallen in love with Celine.

When it had happened, he wasn't absolutely sure. It could have been back in LA when they'd gone to that escape room, or even before that when he'd first laid eyes on her on the stairs. Or maybe it had happened the night she'd shown up at his condo, after successfully escaping from her kidnapper. It didn't matter when it had happened, exactly; the important thing was that it had.

However, there was the biting possibility that she didn't feel the same emotions for him that he felt for her. But as far as he was concerned, if she could do the impossible and make him fall in love with her, then he could certainly do the same and persuade her to fall in love with him.

Before that, though, there was something he had to do, which was to bring closure to what had had him on the run for all these years. It was time he faced the truth, whatever it was, and time he told his father why he'd left the States to move to Rome. His dad had a right to know, and they would handle it together. Zion believed that no matter who his biological father might be, he would always be Langren Blackstone's son. In his heart he believed his father would feel the same way.

After he found closure with his father, Zion planned to go to LA and visit Celine. She'd invited him to do so, but at the time he hadn't been ready to accept her invitation. Now he was.

A crackle of energy passed through him and he knew that he was no longer bound by any rules of his own making. He was now a bachelor unbound and he hoped she was ready for the likes of him.

Leaving his place at the window, he slid into his jeans. Since he wasn't sleepy he wanted to get started making a special piece of gemstone for a certain lady. The woman who'd captured his heart. It would be the most important jewelry he'd ever created.

Celine smiled at Desha. They were finishing up dinner at her favorite restaurant, Andrew's. She had been back in LA for a week and this was the first time she and her best friend had a chance to spend together. First, she had moved out of her father's home. Then word had quickly spread that she was the CEO of Second Chances. The media were clamoring for interviews, trying to find out how she'd kept it a secret for so long. Of course, when they'd contacted her father, he'd pretended to have known all along, refusing to let word get out that she'd kept it from him, as well.

After she filled in her friend on those happenings, they spent the rest of the dinner talking about Zion.

"So there you have it, Desha," she said, as she sat back after confiding everything. "I'm in love."

Desha grinned. "I can see you falling in love with Zion Blackstone. The man is hot."

Celine nodded. "I wanted to tell you I was with him in Rome and why, but couldn't. You would have been the first person my dad contacted about my whereabouts, and I didn't want to put you in the middle of anything."

"No problem, and you're right. When you didn't tell him where you were he began blowing up my phone. I ignored his calls at first because I figured he was the reason you had extended your stay in Rome. That he probably wanted you to do something you didn't want to do, and you were avoiding him. When he kept calling, I finally answered and told him that although I didn't know where you were, you had contacted me to let me know you had decided to extend your time in Rome and that you were okay. I had no idea you were in hiding and he was concerned about you."

Celine rolled her eyes. "He was so concerned with my well-being that he was willing to stage my kidnapping. I'm still upset with him about that."

Desha nodded. "I can't blame you. And I saw the headlines in this morning's paper. You coming out and making a statement that you and Nikon were not engaged and had never been engaged…well, that pretty much called him a liar."

"His problem and not mine."

"Have you heard from Nikon since returning to town?"

Celine took a sip of wine. "He had been blowing up my phone, so I blocked his calls."

"What about Zion? Have you heard from him?"

Celine shook her head sadly. "No, and I don't expect to. I fell in love with him but he didn't fall in love with me. But it doesn't matter. The time I spent with him was special and I will forever have my memories."

"Now who's the liar? It does matter and you know it. This is the first time you've admitted to loving anyone since Jerome. I think you should have told Zion how you felt."

"Doing so would not have served any purpose, Desha. I knew all about his rules."

"But he broke a few for you, right?"

"Yes, but I'm sure he's regretting doing so now," Celine said, taking another sip of her wine.

"What about your father? Is he still mad at you for moving out?"

"Yes. He won't take my calls, and I'm sure after today's headlines he's more angry than ever. I'm happy living in my own place and that's what matters. My happiness. I allowed him to manipulate me for too long."

A short while later, as Desha and Celine were leaving Andrew's, seemingly out of nowhere they were bombarded by paparazzi. Cameras flashed and reporters hollered out questions to Celine, all talking at once.

"Ms. Michaels, is it true that your father and Nikon Anastas arranged for you to be kidnapped to boost their star-power ratings?"

Celine frowned as she kept walking, trying to ignore the mikes being shoved in her face and the cameras flashing in her eyes. "No comment."

"And what about the speculation that you were a part of the plan and hadn't been kidnapped at all?"

Celine slowed her pace for a second, but kept walking, while Desha kept a tight grip on her hand, pulling her on. She wondered if that was the lie those two kidnappers who'd been charged were saying in their defense.

"According to your father, you weren't a part of their plan and you were somewhere hiding out for your safety," said another reporter. "If so, where were you?"

When they reached her car, Desha took the keys from Celine. "Get in," she said. "I'll drive."

Celine was grateful for that, and once she and Desha were in the car with seat belts in place, they sped off.

Chapter 23

"I'm glad you decided to come home, son, and I hope you're planning to stay through the holidays."

Zion glanced across the breakfast table at his father. He had arrived in Atlanta a couple of days ago, after two weeks working on his special piece of jewelry in his cottage in Italy. He'd spent the first day home sleeping off jet lag. Then he had spent as much time as he could with his father. They'd gone to play golf and to pick up a Christmas tree. And he had done something he hadn't done since his mother died—help his father decorate it. He thought the two of them had done a fairly decent job. For as long as Zion could remember, his parents and all their neighbors would kick off the holiday season early by putting up and decorating their trees before Thanksgiving.

"Yes, Dad. My plans are to remain in the States until after New Year's." Possibly even longer than that, if he could convince a certain woman to fall in love with him, he thought.

"Good. That makes me happy."

And more than anything he wanted that for his father. Happiness. Zion had yet to tell his dad what needed to be said. Namely, a secret he didn't want to hide any longer. And he would stay here with his father for as long as it took, to help him get through the news of his wife's betrayal.

"Dad, there's something I need to tell you. It's something I couldn't tell you before now, and because I couldn't I ran off to Rome to live."

His father stopped drinking his coffee and placed his cup down. Concern was etched on Langren Blackstone's face. "What is it, Zion? What could possibly have made you leave your home and the country you love so much?"

Zion glanced over at his father and studied him like he'd done so many times over the past nine years. He'd always looked for some blatant evidence that the man sitting across the table from him was indeed his father and not some no-name guy with whom his mother had engaged in a one-night stand.

"There's a chance I might not be your son, Dad. At least not your biological son." There, he'd said it. The truth was out, and as he continued to watch his father for any sort of reaction, he noticed Langren hadn't even blinked.

"May I ask who told you that lie?"

Although his father's expression remained the same, Zion detected fury in a voice he knew Langren was fighting to keep calm. Zion saw no reason not to tell him the answer, although he wasn't sure it was a lie or not. "Mom told me the last time we talked, while we were at the hospital."

Zion would never forget that day. His mother had deliberately sent his father out of the hospital room, asking for him to check on something with one of her nurses. When Langren had left them she had told Zion that there was a chance, due to a one-night stand she'd engaged in, that Langren was not his biological father.

"Your mother was wrong. You are my biological son." Langren then rubbed the top of his balding head a few times before saying, "And just so you know, I'm fully aware of the affair your mother had with that guy."

Zion's mouth nearly dropped open. "How? Mom said she didn't intend to tell you. That she would take the secret to the grave with her."

"She didn't tell me. I was home when she got in that night. She hadn't expected me to be there, but I had cut my business trip short. She'd been all dressed up, like she had been out for a night on the town. She said she was to meet up with your aunt Darlene, but Darlene canceled at the last minute and your mom decided to go anyway."

Langren paused and added, "Alyse had looked good that night and I immediately knew she had been with someone."

Zion lifted a brow. "How did you know?"

"His scent was still all over her."

Zion didn't say anything. The only thing he could do was to wonder how he would have reacted if he'd come home from a business trip early to discover his wife had been with another man.

"And you didn't question her about it? You actually let her get away with it?"

Langren took a sip of coffee before saying, "Yes. A part of me felt I'd driven her to do what she'd done, Zion. Alyse was a woman who wanted attention. I had gotten so caught up in trying to move to the top of the company, taking assignments I didn't truly need to take, but took anyway. During that time my goal was becoming salesman of the year, not husband of the year, and my marriage suffered."

"But regardless, Dad. That didn't give Mom the right to cheat on you with another man."

Langren remained silent for a moment before he replied. "I loved your mother and I believe she loved me. But that one night, she made a mistake."

Langren paused a minute as if deliberately allowing time for what he'd said to sink in before he continued. "This might be too much information I'm about to share, but under the circumstances I don't believe it is. That night, I suspect your mother wanted to tell me the truth…would have told me the truth. But the minute I realized what she'd done, I swept her into my arms and we showered together. I was intent on erasing that other guy's scent off her. Then I made love to her to wipe away the memory of what she'd done from her mind, as well as my own."

Zion frowned. "And just like that you forgave her?"

Langren leaned back in his chair. "Yes, just like that I forgave her. One day you will understand love, Zion. And when you do, you will know how it is to love someone even with their mistakes. I can tell you, from that day forward, your mother tried being the best wife to me, and I tried being the best husband to her. I wanted to make sure she would never be driven to repeat what she'd done. I accepted my part in her mistake and we moved on."

Zion pondered what his father had said, and then he asked, "What about when you found out she was pregnant? Did you not think that perhaps she was carrying another man's child?"

"Yes, I thought about it, and I would be telling a lie if I said the thought hadn't bothered me at first. But then I decided it didn't matter. Your mother was my wife, whom I loved, and I would love her child regardless of whether I fathered him or not."

Zion had always known his father was a good man.

This proved just how good he was. "So I guess it remains a mystery. Don't you want to know if I'm truly yours?"

Langren stared at him. "You are truly mine, Zion. I am your biological father."

Zion took a sip of his own coffee and then met his father's stare. "How can you be so certain?"

"Because you wear the Blackstone mark."

Zion lifted his brow. "What Blackstone mark?"

"The one on the upper right part of your ass. It was there the last time I changed your diaper and I suspect it's still there."

Zion felt the intense pounding of his heart. "You know about my birthmark?"

Langren chuckled. "Yes. I have one in basically the same place. So did my father and his father. I suspect if you marry, your son will have that same mark, as well."

"Mom never knew."

"I guess she didn't. Since she never confessed to the affair, I never wanted to bring it up. We did talk about how much you favored me while growing up. I assumed it was a foregone conclusion that she knew you were mine. Evidently I was wrong."

"She told me that you thought I was yours, but that she wasn't sure."

"Well, I am sure. I regret that your not knowing was why you fled from home after she died. I couldn't figure out what drove you away. I figured it was grief."

Zion shook his head. "It was partly that, too, but mostly it was my fear of letting something slip that would give her secret away. I didn't want to hurt you."

"Well, now you know it truly wasn't a secret, that I already knew and that I'm more than certain you're my biological son. I regret that Alyse told you anything. It only planted that idea in your head. If you want to do one of those tests to rest your fears, go ahead and waste your money. But you are my son, Zion. I know that the way I knew your mother's secret. I loved her and she loved me. In fact, from that day forward, she told me how she felt about me every day. I knew I was a man loved."

A man loved. Zion wondered at what point a man could be so certain about a woman's feelings for him. Even with his mother's betrayal his father was certain of her love and had forgiven her for her mistake.

"Now that you know the truth, Zion, will you come home more often?"

"Yes, but there's another reason I intend to come home more frequently."

Langren lifted a brow. "What's the reason?"

"I met someone and she lives in California."

A huge smile spread across his father's face. "Who is she? Tell me about her."

Zion was about to do just that when his cell phone rang. It was York. He started to ignore it for the time being, but decided to go ahead and answer it. He hadn't told any of his godbrothers he had returned to the States, but he was certain his father had, since he talked to them pretty regularly.

"This is Y," he said to his father. "If I don't take it, he'll only keep bugging me."

Langren chuckled. "Sounds like something York would do."

Zion clicked on the phone. "What do you want, Y?"

"I figured you haven't been keeping up with the news lately, but you need to turn on the television."

"Why?"

"Just turn on the damn TV, Zion. To that entertainment station." York then ended the call.

Zion wondered what had York so hot under the collar. Standing, he grabbed the remote off the counter to click on the television his father kept in the kitchen. Langren liked watching his sports while cooking.

"There's something York wants me to see on television," he explained to his dad.

Zion switched from ESPN to the entertainment channel. Immediately, his breath left his lungs. There was a picture of Celine plastered across the screen. He turned up the volume.

"So there you have it. The two men Celine Michaels accused of kidnapping her are claiming foul play. They are saying that her father, Levy Michaels, and her fiancé, Nikon Anastas, set up a kidnapping scheme, and that Ms. Michaels was in on the entire thing. They further claim they aren't guilty of kidnapping because at no time was Ms. Michaels held against her will, and that she agreed to spend the entire week with them and could have left at any time. Celine Michaels is denying their statement. But if she wasn't hiding out with her alleged kidnappers, then where was she? Since she refuses to say, we can only doubt her claim."

"Do you know her, Zion?"

Zion clicked off the television and turned to his father. "Yes, I know her. She's the woman I love and she's telling the truth. Those guys did kidnap her and she got away from them."

"And how do you know that?"

Zion drew in a deep breath. "Because when she got away she came to me and was with me, hiding out that week at my home in the country."

"Well, why won't she tell the authorities that?"

He rubbed a hand down his face. "Because she knows how I hate being in the limelight and is trying to protect me."

"Even at the risk of being labeled a liar? At the risk of

kidnappers getting away with a crime they really committed? She sounds to me like a woman trying to protect a man she loves. I guess you're going to have to decide if you love her enough to risk the limelight to protect her."

Zion nodded. "That decision was made before I left Rome, Dad." He placed the remote back on the counter. "I need to fly out to LA for a few days. I promise to be back in time for Thanksgiving, so get the turkey ready."

Celine looked across her desk at her attorney, upset that she had to call in Malcolm to represent her for a case in which she'd clearly been a victim. "So, Mal, what should I do? Regardless of what those men are claiming, I was kidnapped that night, but managed to get away."

Malcolm nodded. "I believe you, but right now it's your word against theirs. They are trying to dodge any jail time and will claim anything. Saying you were a part of your father and Anastas's fake kidnapping scheme will absolve them and all charges would be dropped."

"But I wasn't. Even Dad and Nikon have given statements that I wasn't."

Malcolm nodded. "Yes, but right now the pool of public opinion doesn't believe anything those two are saying. People find it appalling that they would come up with a plan to have their fiancée and daughter kidnapped."

"I understand, because I feel the same way," she said.

"But now that you don't have an alibi—or one you care to share with anyone—it gives reason for people to think you're just as appalling. That is unfortunate, because when news broke that you were the mastermind behind Second Chances, most folks had begun looking at you as the darling of Hollywood."

Celine released a deep sigh. "I don't want to be the darling of Hollywood. I just want to be left alone to run my business. Now that I'm out here, I'm ready to roll up my sleeves and work even harder for Second Chances."

"Well, I hate to tell you this, but those men will keep themselves front and center until you drop those charges."

"I won't drop any charges."

"The Italian officials might be dropping them anyway, without valid proof there was a kidnapping. Why won't you say where you were that week, Celine? Who are you trying to protect?"

At Malcolm's question, the image of Zion flashed in her mind and she couldn't help but smile. All she had were the memories they'd shared, memories she held dear, and she refused to let them be tarnished by those men.

"It doesn't matter. If it ends up being my word against theirs, then fine. I will take my chances."

Malcolm released a deep sigh. "In the meantime, just be prepared for the paparazzi. I understand you're attending that ball tonight."

"Yes, I am." The ball he was referring to was an event to kick off the holiday season for Second Chances. "I won't hide, Malcolm, and I won't drop any charges."

"Then be prepared for the paparazzi tonight. They're relentless and they won't let up until they find out where you were for those seven days."

Celine tried to keep frustration out of her voice when she said, "Let them be relentless. I won't be telling them a thing."

Chapter 24

The limo came to a stop in front of the huge building where the holiday ball for Second Chances was being held. Celine glanced over at Desha and smiled. "Thanks for being my date tonight."

Desha chuckled. "That's what friends are for. Besides, I support you and your causes."

"Thanks." Celine glanced out the window. "Malcolm was right. It seems the paparazzi have doubled in size tonight."

"We'll get through them—don't worry. It will probably be safe just to stick with 'no comment' and keep moving."

"Maybe not. Those two men have been in the news a lot lately, slandering my name. My 'no comment' makes me look guilty."

"Well, unless you're going to tell them about Zion, I would stick to not saying anything. The less information, the better. And speaking of Zion, it's been nearly three and a half weeks. Have you heard anything at all from him?"

A pain pierced Celine's heart. "No."

Desha nodded. "Do you still love him?"

Celine nodded in turn. "I will always love him."

At that moment the chauffeur came around to open the door and Celine whispered to Desha, "Let's hope I get through this."

Zion, decked out in a black-tie ensemble, stood in the shadows and watched as Celine and another woman got out of the limo. The media were everywhere, flashing their cameras and shoving their mikes in Celine's face. And she looked beautiful. The woman he loved looked absolutely gorgeous and at that moment he fell in love with her even more.

He recognized the look in the eyes staring at those reporters. It was her annoyed look. They had begun firing questions at her and she wasn't having it. And frankly, he wasn't, either. Moving forward, he decided it was time to put an end to this madness. And just in time, apparently, when it seemed that one particular reporter was getting on Celine's last nerve.

"If those men are lying," the reporter shouted, his voice rising above the others, "why not tell us where you were? Not doing so makes you appear as guilty in all this as your father and fiancé."

Celine frowned at the man. "What I told all of you was the truth. There was a kidnapping but I got away. And as I've stated a number of times, Nikon and I were never engaged."

"Then where were you for a week? Those guys who you claim kidnapped you are saying you were hiding out with them."

Celine opened her mouth to again refute that, but before she could get her words out, a deep, loud voice boomed from the crowd. "Those men are lying, because Ms. Michaels was with me."

Celine drew in a sharp breath, and heard Desha gasp beside her. Shock took over Celine's entire body. She recognized that voice and stretched her neck to scan the crowd to see where it had come from. Zion was here?

The reporters all turned, as well, searching the crowd to see who had made the comment. Then suddenly, Celine saw him. Everybody saw him when a well-dressed Zion strolled out of the crowd, through the numerous flashing cameras and throng of reporters. And he looked dashing, sexier than she'd ever seen him, dressed in a classic black-and-white tux. But nothing looked classic on him. He stood out, and at that moment was the epitome of everything male. As he walked toward her, his dreadlocks seemed to flow around his shoulders in sync with every sensual step he took.

"Hey, wait a minute," one reporter said to the others. "Isn't that Zion Blackstone? *The* Zion Blackstone, who shuns crowds and publicity of any kind?"

"It looks like him," another reporter said, and others among the crowd began whispering his name. "His home is in Rome. Is he claiming that Ms. Michaels was with him those seven days?"

Zion came to a stop in front of Celine amid a storm of flashing lights. "Hello, sweetheart," he said in greeting, before leaning in and placing an extended kiss on her lips. One that seemed to leave no doubt in anyone's mind the nature of their relationship. It also gave the reporters time to snap several pictures of the kiss.

"Zion?" she said, clearly surprised to see him.

He smiled before taking a place at her side. A place Celine noted that Desha gladly gave up to him. Zion took her hand in his and then turned to face the mass of reporters and the cameras. "Since Celine was with me for those seven days, you are free to ask me anything."

With that invitation, the reporters began firing their questions. Zion grinned and held up a finger. "One at a time, please." He nodded at the man directly in front of him.

That reporter asked, "Are you substantiating Ms. Michaels's claim that she was kidnapped?"

"I am. She escaped them and came straight to me, where she remained in my care and under my protection for seven days."

"You have proof of that?" another reporter questioned.

Zion nodded. "I most certainly do. As you all probably know, I live in a very secured condo. Records are kept and videos are made. If needed I could verify the time she arrived and the fact that she did arrive. I can also verify that she was with me when we left for my home in the country the next day."

Voices buzzed through the crowd. Celine stood there, amazed at how aptly Zion was handling the media. He might prefer not dealing with them, but he definitely knew how to control the narrative. Not only did he look dashing, he also exuded an air of sophistication and charm.

"Do you have proof of any of this? It will be your and Ms. Michaels's words against the kidnappers."

"No problem. Once I discovered what happened to Celine, I immediately hired a top-notch security company to find those men. That wasn't hard to do since they were parked outside her hotel, hoping she would return. The security detail I hired kept those men within view until the time they were arrested. Their comings and goings were captured on video and at no time was Celine with them. Like I said, she was with me."

"Then why didn't she just say that?" one reporter asked, as if in frustration.

Zion switched his gaze from the reporters to Celine. "Celine knows how much I abhor the limelight and did it to protect me. But what she didn't know, and what I evidently didn't make clear to her, is that she means more to me than avoiding any limelight."

"Are you saying you're in love with Ms. Michaels, Mr. Blackstone?"

Zion recognized the voice. It was his friend from college whom he'd arranged to be in the crowd to ask that very question. He looked out into the sea of reporters. "Yes, that's exactly what I'm saying." He then turned his attention back to Celine. "I love you."

Tears were streaming down her face and Desha shoved a napkin in her hand to dab her eyes before ruining her makeup. "And I love you, too, Zion."

Zion, surprised yet pleased with her words, pulled her into his arms and kissed her, not caring that the cameras flashed again.

When he finally released her mouth he heard a reporter ask, "Does this mean she'll be getting a ring by Zion?"

Zion turned to the crowd with a huge smile on his face. "Yes, Celine will definitely be getting a ring by Zion when I ask for her hand in marriage in a more private setting. Now if you all will excuse us, we have a party to attend and, hopefully soon, an engagement to celebrate."

Taking Celine's hand in his, Zion led her inside the building.

It was after midnight when Celine led Zion into her apartment. The night had been wonderful and Zion had remained by her side the entire time. Word had quickly spread that Zion had been the person she'd spent her week in Italy with, and that they had declared their love for each other in front of the paparazzi. No doubt it would make tomorrow's headlines.

To Celine's surprise, her father had attended the event. He'd thanked Zion for protecting his daughter while she'd been in Rome and told him he was glad Zion had come forward with proof that she hadn't been involved in the kidnapping. And once again he'd apologized to Celine, saying it was never his intent to put her in harm's way.

In all, it had been a good party. And now she was looking forward to an even better night.

"Nice place," Zion commented as he entered her apartment.

Celine removed her wrap as he looked around. "Thanks. Would you like something to drink?"

He nodded. "Coffee would be nice and then we need to talk, Celine."

Yes, they did. "I'll be back in a minute."

When Celine returned, Zion had removed his jacket and was standing by the window, looking out as if he belonged there. He turned when she entered the living room, and nothing had changed. They still shared a potent sexual chemistry.

"Here you are," she said, setting the tray she held down on the table before handing a cup to him.

"Thanks."

"You said we needed to talk," she said, picking up her own cup and heading to the sofa. He took the chair across from her.

"Yes. I took your advice about ridding myself of all that negative wasted energy. When I did, I discovered a lot of things about myself."

"Such as?"

"I could finally let go of something that has plagued

me for years. Something that drove me to live in Rome and kept me there."

He then shared everything with her. His mother's death-bed confession and, more recently, his conversation with his father. "I found closure, Celine."

"I am so happy for you, Zion. I am glad you know the truth and that you are your father's son."

"I'm glad, too. Now I wish I had gone to Dad in the be-ginning, but I don't regret the year I spent traveling abroad with York, and the eight years I've lived in Rome. What I do regret is the times I could have come home and didn't."

Celine nodded. "I want to thank you for standing up for me tonight. I'm glad you felt comfortable in letting ev-eryone know I was with you. And I didn't know York had someone tailing those guys."

"I didn't feel the need to tell you until I discovered those men were trying to make you into a coconspirator instead of a victim. York will be turning his report over to the Ital-ian authorities. Trust me, he's very thorough and the footage he obtained will discount their story. And you don't have to thank me for anything. As long as there is life within me, I will always be ready to protect the woman I love."

Celine's heart began pumping. "The woman you love?" He'd said it before, in front of everyone. Now she wanted to hear him say it again, just for her.

"Yes, I said it and I meant it. I love you." He placed his cup on the table next to his chair, stood and came over to her. Taking her cup from her, as well, he placed it on the coffee table by the sofa. Then he got down on a bended knee and took her hand.

"I'll settle for a long engagement if that's what you want. But what I want, what I need, is to have you in my life. For-ever. Celine, will you marry me?"

Love and excitement spread through Celine. She was

so blinded by her tears that she didn't see the ring box he'd pulled out of his pocket until she wiped her eyes. Then it was there in his hand, the diamond's brilliance almost blinding her. She caught her breath at the ring's beauty. OMG! She was so taken by the striking design of the ring that she could barely get out the words. "Yes, I'll marry you."

Zion smiled broadly. "I designed this ring especially for you," he said, sliding it on her finger. "That's what I've been up to for the past few weeks."

Celine glanced down at her hand. This ring by Zion was absolutely stunning. As stunning as the man who'd slipped it on her finger. "Oh, Zion. It's absolutely beautiful. I love it and I love you."

Pulling her up from the sofa, he wrapped her in his arms. "And I love you."

He lowered his mouth to hers for a kiss—one that would be the first of many, she knew. And she was more than ready for the kisses and anything else he had in mind.

Tonight and always.

Epilogue

Seven months later

On the night before Zion's wedding, at the end of his bachelor party, six men remained when everyone else returned to their hotel rooms. Together, after removing their shoes, they headed out toward the beach.

Zion and Celine had decided on a June destination wedding in Jamaica. Celine was staying at one hotel and Zion at another. Tomorrow at noon, the wedding would take place at a church on the island. Zion hadn't seen Celine since he'd arrived yesterday. She had warned him that she intended to stay hidden until the wedding, and he couldn't wait to see her walk down the aisle to him.

The kidnapping incident had been resolved. With York's proof, the abductors had been charged with the crime, and both Levy and Anastas were required to do many hours of community service. The two men definitely had gotten a lot of publicity over the past few months. Unfortunately, it hadn't been the kind they'd wanted.

Celine had finally accepted her father's apology and he would be walking her down the aisle tomorrow. Zion also knew Levy had made several statements in the press about how proud he was of his daughter and her role at Second Chances. According to Celine, he'd even made a huge donation to the foundation. That was certainly a start.

Celine's birthday had been a huge success. She had loved the birthday gift her father had given her, the necklace and earrings by Zion. She said she loved both pieces even more because he'd created them for her. It made Zion feel proud each and every time she wore the jewelry. He thought both looked perfect with her engagement ring.

The six men—all godbrothers—came to a stop in front of a roaring firepit. "Okay, guys, you know what we need to do," Uriel Lassiter said, snagging Zion's attention.

Yes, they knew. The six of them had formed the Bachelors in Demand Guarded Hearts Club and now it was time to end it. Five of them were happily married and Zion would take the plunge tomorrow. Although their friends Mercury and Gannon Steele, as well as a few other single acquaintances, had expressed an interest in joining the club, no one had submitted a membership application.

"The club did serve its purpose for a while," Virgil Bougard said.

"But then we met the loves of our lives and the rest is history," Xavier Kane added.

Zion nodded. Virgil and Xavier were right. The rest was history. Zion had been left as the lone member after the others had defected, and he'd pledged to keep the club going. But that had been before meeting Celine. Tomorrow, he would be saying vows that would bind her to him forever and he couldn't wait.

She had spent the holidays with him and had gotten to meet Zion's father, the godfathers, godbrothers and all the wives. Everyone loved Celine and thought the woman who'd captured Zion's heart was worthy of his love.

The two of them had decided to make their primary home in Atlanta, to be close to Langren. They would keep both Zion's places in Rome and Celine's in LA. Being in Atlanta provided them with direct flights to California when she needed to check on her father and Second Chances.

"You guys ready?" Winston Coltrane asked, interrupting Zion's thoughts. Winston and his wife, Ainsley, had welcomed their firstborn, a son they'd named Warrick. Zion would be the first to admit the kid looked just like Winston. And York and Darcy had a beautiful little girl they'd named Keir. She had both York's and Darcy's features. More of Darcy's, thank God.

"Ready," the others said simultaneously. They began feeding pages of the club's charter into the fire to burn them to ashes, never to rise again. When the last page had burned, the godbrothers glanced around at each other, smiled and nodded. The Guarded Hearts Club was no more. They were no longer Bachelors in Demand. By this time tomorrow, all six would be happily married men.

They began walking back toward the hotel, declaring a glass of scotch was in order when they got there.

The wedding day

"Zion and Celine, I now pronounce you husband and wife. Zion, you may kiss your bride," the minister said.

Celine turned to Zion after Desha pushed back her veil. She couldn't help but smile up at the man who'd broken all his rules for her. The man who had offered her his protection and then his love. The man who was happily sharing his godfathers and godmothers with her. Now she'd inherited five godbrothers and their wives. She, Ellie Lassiter, Darcy Ellis, Farrah Kane, Kara Bougard and Ainsley Coltrane had quickly become the best of friends.

"Pucker up, Mrs. Blackstone. Mr. Blackstone is about to brand you his forever," Zion whispered against her lips.

And then he kissed her, and boy, did he kiss her. She could hear all the cheering, catcalls and applause, but Zion kept right on kissing her. And she kept right on kissing him back, while settling deeper into his possessive embrace.

She couldn't think of any other way for them to start the rest of their lives together.

* * * * *

Soulful and sensual romance featuring multicultural characters.

Look for brand-new Kimani stories
in special 2-in-1 volumes starting March 2019.

Available March 5, 2019

LOVE IN SAN FRANCISCO & UNCONDITIONALLY
by Shirley Hailstock and Janice Sims

A TASTE OF PASSION & AMBITIOUS SEDUCTION
by Chloe Blake and Nana Prah

**PLEASURE AT MIDNIGHT & HIS PICK
FOR PASSION**
by Pamela Yaye and Synithia Williams

**BECAUSE YOU LOVE ME & JOURNEY TO
MY HEART**
by Monica Richardson and Terra Little

www.Harlequin.com

KPST1218

Get 4 FREE REWARDS!

We'll send you 2 FREE Books
<u>plus</u> 2 FREE Mystery Gifts.

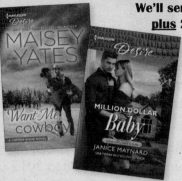

Harlequin® Desire books feature heroes who have it all: wealth, status, incredible good looks... everything but the right woman.

FREE Value Over **$20**

Once she'd heard the rumor about Singleton Financial
wanting to find another firm to represent their conglomeration,
she'd dived for their information. After being trusted to
work with them—although with Leonardo—within the past
year, she felt obligated to encourage them to stay. What had
happened to make them want to leave? It couldn't have been
the work she and Leonardo had done for them; they'd been
happy customers two months ago.

She wouldn't focus on what else had transpired during
that time, but her skin heated at the memory that was trying

to make its way to the forefront of her mind. Soon she'd be face-to-face with the man she'd been avoiding. They'd never been friends, so it hadn't been that hard to stay away. And yet her body still betrayed her on a daily basis and longed for the boar's touch.

Shaking off the biggest mistake of her life, she zoned in on her career. If she could maintain Singleton Financial as a client, she'd definitely be made partner. No way would she allow the muscle-bound Astacio to snatch the chance away from her.

Once again she wondered why he even worked for the firm. His family possessed more money than Oprah Winfrey and Bill Gates combined. He could've gone to work for his family, started his own law firm or even retired. Jealousy roared to life at how easy his life had been.

A buzz from her phone brought her out of her musings just in time to prepare her for the bear who banged her poor door against the wall before storming in. Their erotic encounter hadn't changed him a bit.

Canting her head, she presented a smile sweet enough for him to develop cavities. "How may I help you, Leonardo?" For a rather uptight law firm, they held an open policy about calling people by their first names, although most of the employees called him Mr. Astacio out of terror. She'd rather scrub toilets at an office building again, a job she'd had in high school.

He stopped in front of her desk and braced his hands on it. "You have something that belongs to me."

A thrill shimmied down her spine at being so close to him. Ignoring the way his baritone voice sounded even huskier than normal, she looked around her shared office, glad to find they were alone so they could fight toe-to-toe. "What's that?"

"Don't play games." He pointed to his chest, about to speak again, when an adorable sneeze slipped out. Followed by four more. So the big bad wolf had a cold. From the gossip mill, she knew he never got sick. Detested doing so.

She got to her feet and walked around her desk to the door. She used it as a fan to air the room out. "Since I can't open the windows, I'd prefer if you didn't share your nasty germs with me."

His clenched, broad jaw didn't scare her. Especially considering how his upturned nose now held a tinge of red after blowing it. The man had a monopoly on sexy with his large dark brown eyes and sharp cheekbones. His tailored suit hugged a muscular body she'd jump hurdles to get reacquainted with if he wasn't such an arrogant ass. *And my competition for financial freedom. Mustn't forget that.*

Leonardo held out his hand. "Hand over the file. It's mine."

She'd worn her favorite suit to work, so she had an extra dose of power on her side. Although her outfit wasn't tailored like his, she'd spent more money on the form-flattering dark plum skirt suit than she had on three of her others combined. Kamilla perched a hand on her hip and hitched her upper body forward in a challenge. "Who says?"

"I do."

Tapping her finger against her chin, she shrugged. "Well, that's all the verification I need. I'll give it to you." She sashayed to her desk and sat on the edge. "Right after I'm finished analyzing it."

Don't miss Ambitious Seduction
by Nana Prah, available March 2019
wherever Harlequin® Kimani Romance™
books and ebooks are sold.

Want to give in to temptation with
steamy tales of irresistible desire?

Check out **Harlequin® Presents®,
Harlequin® Desire** and
Harlequin® Kimani™ Romance books!

New books available every month!

CONNECT WITH US AT:

Facebook.com/groups/HarlequinConnection

Facebook.com/HarlequinBooks

Twitter.com/HarlequinBooks

Instagram.com/HarlequinBooks

Pinterest.com/HarlequinBooks

ReaderService.com

**ROMANCE WHEN
YOU NEED IT**

PGENRE2018